DEATH UNDER THE ICE

Trouble in Pleasant Valley • Book Four

Deborah Sprinkle

Scrivenings
PRESS
Quench your thirst for story.
www.ScriveningsPress.com

Published by Scrivenings Press LLC
15 Lucky Lane
Morrilton, Arkansas 72110
https://ScriveningsPress.com

Printed in the United States of America

Paperback ISBN 978-1-64917-434-5

eBook ISBN 978-1-64917-435-2

Editors: Suzie Waltner and Heidi Glick

Cover design by Linda Fulkerson - www.bookmarketinggraphics.com

All characters are fictional, and any resemblance to real people, either factual or historical, is purely coincidental.

To Doug, our talented and kind son

1

No lights shone from the house. Not even the porch light. Homeland Security Agent Claire Green turned her back to the cold wind and leaned on the doorbell again. After a few minutes with no response, she slogged through the snow to the garage and entered the code.

The garage door creaked and groaned as it rose. Claire ducked under when it was waist-high. Alan's gray SUV stood to one side. She removed her glove and placed a hand on the hood. Ice cold. She peered through the windows of the vehicle. Nothing out of place.

If her brother had locked the interior door, she'd break in. But the knob turned easily in her hand, and she stepped inside. "Alan?" No answer. She laid her purse on the counter by the sink and walked farther into the house. Even though the house was warm, the abode had a deserted feel that made her edgy. It wasn't like Alan to call her in a panic about something, demand she help him, and then forget all about it.

She moved through her brother's rental home, turning on lights and searching everywhere—including closets. When she got to his room, his heavy coat, the one he always wore, lay on his bed, along with his gloves and hat. Something was definitely up. He'd never go out in weather like this without them. She chewed on her lip and willed herself to stay calm. After all, she hadn't seen him in months. Was it possible he had another coat?

Knowing Alan as she did, the idea of him buying another coat when his old one was still good wasn't likely, but the other possibilities were too terrible to consider. On the other hand, she'd found no signs of a struggle or traces of blood. So maybe he did own two coats?

One more place to look. She retraced her steps to the garage. An old chest freezer stood in front of his SUV. She took a deep breath. "You can do this."

Claire closed her eyes and lifted the lid with a trembling hand. If she still believed in prayer, she would have said one now, but she'd long since realized her supplication did no good. A blast of frosty air hit her face and froze her breath. She opened her eyes and exhaled. No Alan. Only packages wrapped in white butcher paper, stacked in a bin on the left. Her knees gave, and she leaned on the rim until the cold seeped into her bones. She slammed the top shut and, shivering, fled back to the warmth of the house.

After pulling her car into the garage and unloading her suitcases, Claire fixed herself something to eat. "The fridge is stocked." She had a habit of thinking out loud, which drove her colleagues nuts, and her mom and dad before them. "He was ready for my visit." A clot of fear formed in her throat, making it hard to swallow. "Where are you, Alan?"

Had he forgotten when she was due to arrive? Not likely. Maybe he'd gone out with someone and couldn't get home or contact her, but that didn't make much sense either. "One more search before I let myself get worried."

A more thorough search yielded a few items Claire placed on the kitchen table—his appointment diary, an old photo of him with his police pals, a map of Ohio she'd found tucked back in a drawer, and a key. But no cellphone or computer. She wasn't sure why she'd collected those things, but she trusted her instincts.

She tried calling Alan's cellphone, but it wouldn't go through. Maybe he *had* gone out and couldn't get in touch with her after all. She picked up the appointment book and moved across the great room to his recliner. The house seemed like it always did, but something prodded at the sixth sense she'd developed after years on the job. She surveyed the room.

Curtains covered the wall of windows looking out on Lake Pleasant. She let her gaze linger on the antique oak buffet that stood against the far-left wall. Claire had often admired that piece with the wide mirror hanging above it. A long oak dining table with mismatched chairs took up most of the space in front of it.

Closer to where she stood, Alan's old leather recliner rested on a large area rug with a sturdy end table beside it and a floor lamp on the other side. Across the room from his chair, tall bookcases flanked the fireplace with a big screen television mounted above the mantle. A sofa rounded out the furniture on this end of the room. All the furniture came with the house except her brother's chair.

Nothing seemed out of place. With a sigh, Claire grabbed a soft, beige throw and curled into the recliner with the appointment book in her lap. "Let's see what you've been up to, Alan."

Deciphering her brother's chicken scratch and shorthand proved too much for her distracted brain and worried heart. She closed the book and tilted the chair back. The piece of furniture cushioned her like a big hug, and she understood now why he dragged this recliner with him wherever he lived. The stressful drive through winter weather and concern for her brother left her drained. Her eyes closed.

A RAY of sunlight lasered through a slit in the curtains and lit up the inside of Claire's eyelids. She grunted, stretched, and banged her arm into the lamp on her left. "What the ..." She tried to swing her legs out of bed before remembering she was in Alan's recliner. "Oh, man. Alan, on second thought, I don't like your chair."

After wrestling the recliner to its upright position, she rose and folded the throw into a square before adding it to the pile in a basket near the hearth. Alan bordered on obsessive. There were no useless decorations in his house, and once he decided on a place for something, it never changed. A blind person would have no problem navigating her brother's house.

She opened the drapes on the floor-to-ceiling windows and gazed out on a winter scene right off a Christmas card. The December sun turned the blanket of pristine snow covering the yard and thirty-acre lake beyond into a field of diamonds.

"Wow. I see why you love it here, bro." Claire turned away from the view. Her chest ached to see him in his chair or at the kitchen sink washing dishes. "Where are you, Alan?"

Once more, she felt that pinch to the intuition she'd honed over the years. "Aargh. What am I missing?" His appointment book caught her eye, and as she retrieved it, she noticed the marks on the rug where the table normally stood. "Why would you move your table?" She explored the dents with her fingers. Even if he cleaned the rug, he'd be careful to place the furniture back where it had rested before. That's how Alan was wired.

She moved to the bookcases. The fine hairs on the back of her neck stood on end. Some of the books were upside down, and they weren't in alphabetical order. She reached to touch them but stopped.

There was one more place she needed to check. Claire hurried to Alan's bedroom and flung open his closet door. Her brother always hung his clothes in a certain order from left to right. T-shirts first, jeans, his two dress shirts, dress pants, his sports coats, and his one suit.

And there it was. The evidence she needed to convince herself. Shirts together, pants together. Alan would never deviate from the pattern he'd used his entire adult life.

Someone had searched her brother's house. Someone who thought they'd covered their tracks. But who? And what were they looking for?

2

———————

"What have you gotten yourself into, Alan?" Claire backed up and sat on her brother's bed. "You're not off somewhere with a friend. You're in trouble." Her eyes roamed over the sparse furniture in the bedroom. "But why would someone searching your house bother to try to put things back the way they were?"

She couldn't cope with whatever this was, alone. But who could she trust to help? Not her co-workers at Homeland Security. If her brother was involved in something he shouldn't be, she didn't want to incriminate him, nor did she want to jeopardize her job. At least not until she discovered what her brother was involved in first.

The sound of footsteps on the front porch interrupted her thoughts. She jumped up and reached for her weapon, only to remember she'd left it with her suitcase in the guest room upstairs. "How could you be so stupid?" She inched down the hall toward the front of the house, her back against the wall. Shadows flickered across the frosted window adjacent to the front door. She jerked as a bell chimed above her head.

"Alan, are you in there? It's Madison."

Her brother had spoken of a couple he'd become friends

7

with. Madison and ... she couldn't remember the man's name. Claire cracked the door open and braced it with her body. A large black dog stuck his nose in and tried to lick her face.

"Oscar, no." The woman's light brown hair fell forward. She brushed it behind her ears and gave Claire a warm smile. "I'm Madison Zuberi. We live next door."

"I'm Claire, Alan's sister." The corners of her mouth lifted in response. She couldn't help it. Something was engaging about this woman.

"It's nice to meet you." Madison's face brightened. "Alan's told us so much about you. He says you are the smartest person he's ever known."

Alan had told them about her? She relaxed her stance, and Oscar must have seen that as a welcome gesture. Next thing she knew, he pushed between her and the door and bolted into the house.

"No." Madison threw out her hands, eyes wide with embarrassment. "Get back here pronto, mister."

Claire opened the door wider and bit her lip to keep from laughing as the dog slunk back down the hall.

"I'm sorry. He doesn't usually misbehave like this." Madison clipped a leash on Oscar's collar. "I came over to invite Alan to dinner this evening. We'd love to have you join us as well."

"I ..." She studied Madison. Maybe this was one of those rare times when things happen for a reason. "Do you have a moment?"

Madison glanced at Oscar.

"It's okay. He can come in."

"I'll keep him on his leash." Madison stepped onto the rug inside the door. "Oscar, sit."

"I know this sounds crazy." Claire shoved her hands into the pockets of her sweater. "But I think something's happened to Alan."

"From what he's shared about you, I doubt you're crazy," Madison said. "Go on."

"When I got here last night, I thought maybe he'd gone out with a friend and couldn't get home or in touch with me." Claire rubbed the spot on her forehead between her eyes where a headache threatened. "But this morning, I realized it's more than that. He's missing, and I'm not sure why."

"Claire, I'm sorry." Madison's amber eyes darkened. "We're happy to help in any way we can. Let me give you my number." She pulled a card out of her pocket and handed it to Claire. "The dinner invitation still stands. Nate will be home around five, but feel free to come over anytime."

RPI, Forensic Investigator, Madison Long Zuberi. "You're a private eye?"

"Sort of." Madison gave her a shy smile. "My husband, Nate, is the big gun. He's captain of the Pleasant Valley police force."

Claire nodded. She'd found help, but would it end up costing her brother his reputation?

* * *

MADISON RELEASED her dog and slogged through the snow toward home. It had been a long time—years—since she'd been involved in a serious case. Mostly because she'd had the twins.

Oscar gave a vigorous shake at the back door, sending wet snow flying everywhere.

"Thanks for that, dog." She snorted a laugh and wiped her face. "At least you didn't wait until we were inside." In the past few years, they'd made improvements to their house. One was to convert their screened porch to all-season.

She gazed at the four pairs of ice skates sitting next to the door, two large and two small, and her heart swelled with gratitude for the one big person and two little people who wore them. Normally, the twins would be home from pre-kindergarten at about three in the afternoon and ready to hit the ice out back. But not today, and she was glad to have something take her focus away from how much she missed them.

She'd start a file on Alan Green and record the conversations they'd had in the last six months. A wave of excitement mixed with a shred of guilt ran through her. She didn't wish her friendly neighbor harm, but the idea of using her brain for something more than playing educational video games thrilled her. She grabbed her electronic notepad and settled into the new recliner in their enlarged living room/den.

The question remained. Was she ready to take on a major investigation again? She rubbed the silver filigree cross that hung around her neck. With His help, she knew she could.

Her phone rang, and her husband's handsome appeared on the screen. "Nate, I was just thinking about you."

"I was thinking about you too."

The low, soft tones of his voice still made her tingle inside, even after six years of marriage.

"Did you talk to Alan?" he asked. "Is he able to come for dinner?"

She paused, unsure how to tell him about her news. "Alan's sister, Claire, is at his house."

"Good. She can come too."

"She is, but Alan's missing. I told her we would help find him."

"Is she certain? Do you think she's, you know, reliable?"

"Nate, she's an analyst for Homeland Security. I think she knows what she's talking about."

"Sorry. You're right."

"I'm going through our conversations with her brother over the last six months—what I can remember—and making notes. I'll need your help since you two did most of the talking."

"Good idea. What about Rafe?"

"I'll call him. I love you."

"Love you more."

Her husband's call came at the perfect time. She set to work with renewed focus. Since Nate and Alan shared a law enforcement background, most of their conversations centered on their work. She'd listened but hadn't caught everything as she served dinner or cleared away dishes. Nate would have to fill in the gaps.

Alan talked a lot about three close friends and the pranks they played on each other. They all left the force about the same time and went their separate ways.

One day, she'd asked Alan if he was still in touch with them. He looked down at his coffee and said, "Sort of." Then changed the subject.

Madison recorded the incident and added a question about what happened to his friends. Where were they now? Did they have a falling out? Was it one or all of them?

She filled five pages with snatches of memories and questions before breaking for lunch. Oscar stood at the kitchen window, gazing at the snowy playground outside. He loved this weather. She squatted beside him and grabbed him by the scruff of his neck. "Hey, big guy. We'll go out and test the ice after I eat."

Oscar caught the word "out," and his ears perked up. Madison gave him a treat and fixed herself a sandwich. After inhaling the morsel, the black lab perched beside her chair and stared at her with big brown eyes.

"You know that doesn't work with me." She glared. "I'm not going to rush my lunch. You can wait."

Oscar sighed and collapsed onto the floor, head on his paws. But as soon as she pushed back her chair, he jumped to his feet and trotted to the back door.

Madison chuckled. "You're as bad as the kids." She washed her hands and headed for the porch.

A breeze almost always blew across the open stretch of ice, carrying with it bits of frozen snow that penetrated her jeans and stung her face. She took the time to pull on ski pants and her heavy boots, along with her parka and gloves.

She grabbed her skates, a snow shovel, and a long-handled pick to test the ice. The first blast of cold air took her breath away, but Oscar raced across the deck and down the steps as if it were spring. He buried his nose in the snow, flung it upward, and snapped at it in his own private game. "I wish I had your energy," she said to herself. "Or felt that joy."

Lately, Madison had begun to question her purpose in life. Was she meant to keep the house, look after the kids, and be Nate's wife? Was that all for her? Part of her wanted more, and the other part felt guilty because she'd been so blessed. How horrible that the disappearance of Alan Green got her blood pumping with excitement.

She reached the end of the yard and stepped out onto the ice. Every day, she scraped away a ten-to-fifteen-foot semicircle of snow around the dock. When the twins got home, she took them skating. Today, it was only her. She'd come to enjoy the exercise. Sweat trickled down her back as she worked, but she knew better than to take off her jacket. That was a good way to let her core body temperature get too low.

Oscar abandoned his game and padded onto the ice, sniffing the surface.

"What are you doing, dog?" Madison paused while putting on her skates.

At the far edge of the cleared section, he stiffened, nose to the ice. The hair on the back of his neck stood up, and he uttered a menacing growl low in his throat.

3

Madison only heard a growl like that from him one other time. The sweat along her back turned to icicles. She glided over to him.

Through the opaque ice, she saw what looked like a dead carp pressed against the underside of the frozen water. She dropped to her knees and wrapped her arms around her dog's neck.

"It's a fish, you big lug." She buried her face in his fur and willed her heart to stop racing. "Only a fish this time."

He licked her cheek.

"Okay." She rose and surveyed the makeshift skating rink. A few more trips around the ice and then back to the house. Years had passed since the day she'd stumbled upon the body of her former boyfriend by the lake. Things were a lot different then. She turned her feet and scraped to a halt, sending ice particles spraying. Now, she was a private investigator.

And it was time for this private eye to fix dinner. She uttered a quick laugh.

MADISON MOVED around the scarred oak table, distributing silverware and straightening placemats. It had been a while since they'd had someone new to the house for dinner. The aroma of simmering beef mixed with roasted potatoes and carrots—with an undertone of yeasty rolls baking in the oven—made her mouth water and her stomach growl.

A simple and hearty meal that everyone seemed to enjoy. She put a hand to her mouth. Unless Claire was a vegetarian. Did she have the ingredients for a salad?

Oscar scrambled to his feet and let out a single woof. Someone was at the door. Madison wiped her hands on a towel and maneuvered through the dining room to where her dog stood with his nose against the door and his tail whipping back and forth. Rafe, her boss and friend, must be on the porch.

Madison gave her dog's ear a gentle shake. "You're supposed to love me best, remember?"

He turned sad brown eyes on her and let out a pitiful whine.

"I give up." She opened the door and stepped back to allow him time to say hello.

Oscar pawed at their visitor and barked. Rafe rubbed the dog's big head. "Where are the little people?"

"The twins are on a trip with Gran and Gramps." Nate walked in from the hallway, his hair damp and smelling of soap. "Hi, buddy." He shook hands with Rafe.

"Sounds like fun for the kids." Rafe O'Connell glanced at Madison. "Where are they going?"

"Nate's parents are taking them to his uncle's seventieth birthday party in Philadelphia." Madison herded the men farther inside. "Nate can't get away from work, and I didn't want to go without him. But his parents asked if they could take the kids so the rest of the family can meet them."

"And you two might get some much-deserved time to yourselves."

"That would be nice." She let out a small sigh. Somehow, she doubted that would be the case.

"Who's the fourth person?" Rafe lifted his gaze from the extra place setting and narrowed his eyes at her. "You're not playing matchmaker again, are you?"

"No. Although she is cute." She threw him a quick grin. "She's your tenant's sister. She came to visit her brother and found the house empty."

"Empty, huh?" Rafe walked over to the kitchen windows. Something she'd said tugged at his memory. He rubbed his chin. What was it?

"His car's in the garage, and his coat and gloves on the bed." Madison pulled the rolls out of the oven. "She needs our help, and since you're my boss and his landlord, I thought you might want to be a part of this."

"Why not?" He gave a half-hearted shrug. "We don't have much going on right now."

"Madison, I need you in the bedroom for a minute." Nate motioned to his wife.

She covered the food. "If she arrives before I get back, let her in, will you?"

Oscar raised his head and woofed low in his throat.

"I think your mommy planned this." Rafe scrubbed his fist on top of Oscar's head and strode to the front door.

"I hate coming to dinner without a gift, but ..." The woman stepped into the house, threw back her parka hood, and unwound her scarf before looking up. "Rafe?"

"Claire." His chest constricted at the sight of the riot of auburn waves. That was it. When they were together, he'd met Alan briefly. He should have made the connection when Madison mentioned Alan's sister. Why hadn't it occurred to him it would be Claire?

Because he'd worked hard to forget the woman standing before him.

"There you are." Madison smiled at her. "Let me get your coat. Rafe, would you please close the door?" She gave him a pointed look.

He took his time securing the door. If Madison had told him Claire Green was coming to dinner, he would have thought of an excuse and left before she got here. Now, he had no choice but to spend the evening in the presence of the only woman he'd ever loved but who'd broken his heart.

"I feel terrible about spilling my guts to you like I did. Alan's probably off with some of his buddies and forgot I was coming." Claire replaced her scarf and zipped up her parka. "I think I'll pass on dinner tonight. But thanks for the invitation."

"Nonsense. I've been cooking all day, and it's ready." Madison put her hands on her hips and peered from Rafe to Claire and back. "You two know each other, don't you? Is that why you're so anxious to leave?"

"Look. If anybody's going to leave, it should be me." A flush of heat traveled up his neck and into his cheeks. He squared his shoulders. "She needs your help."

"And yours." Madison pierced him with her gaze.

"Dinner and the details. That's it," he said through gritted teeth. Madison knew he couldn't resist a puzzle. It was like an itch he had to scratch. He would do this for Madison and Nate. The two of them and the twins were the closest thing he had to family.

"Good. Let's eat."

Rafe let the women lead the way to the kitchen and took his usual place with his back to the blue antique cupboard. A pang of jealousy hit him as Nate welcomed Claire into their home. He scrubbed a hand down his face. Get a grip, O'Connell.

"I think that's it." Madison set the last dish on the table and pulled out her chair.

"It smells wonderful." Claire leaned in and took a deep breath. "It's been a while since I've had a home-cooked meal."

"I'll say the blessing, and we can dig in." Nate folded his hands.

As his friend thanked God for the food, Rafe couldn't resist looking out from under lowered lids at the woman across the table. Claire sat with her hands in her lap. After a moment, she raised clouded emerald eyes to his, and despite the years, his heart lurched in his chest.

Rafe admired the way Madison kept the dinner conversation light and put them all at ease. Her intuition about people never ceased to amaze him. She even managed to make him feel relaxed. After clearing the table, they regrouped with coffee and tea.

"Why don't you tell us what happened and why you're worried," Nate said.

"Madison has already heard this, but here goes." Claire related how she'd arrived, went in through the garage, and what she found inside. "Something seemed off, but I couldn't put my finger on what. It wasn't until the next morning I realized things weren't where Alan kept them." She told them about her brother's obsessive habits and how she realized the house had been searched.

"That sounds like a police search or one done by the feds." Nate furrowed his brow. "Doesn't it to you?"

"Now that you point it out, it does." Claire leaned back in her chair. "But why would they be searching my brother's house? He's been retired for five years."

"No moonlighting?" Rafe asked. How would his ex-girlfriend know how the feds searched a house?

"I don't think so." She bit her lip. "He would have told me."

"You see him a lot?" If that were the case, why hadn't he seen her before now?

"No, but we talk every week."

"Not the same. He could be speaking to you from anywhere." Rafe ran a hand down his face. "Maybe he didn't want you to know what he was up to."

"True. But he begged me to come." She nodded. "If he had to leave on an assignment, why didn't he let me know his plans had changed? And why did he leave without his coat?"

Good questions, and Rafe vowed to find the answers.

4

———

"Did your brother keep a diary or journal of any kind? Maybe a calendar?" Madison looked across the kitchen table at Claire, hoping for a place to start.

"Yes." Claire rose and returned with a large handbag she'd left in the other room. "I've been trying to decipher his handwriting and his shorthand, but I haven't gotten very far." She laid the appointment book on the table.

"May I look at it?" Madison asked.

"Sure. I also found this key. I think it's to a safe deposit box."

"Yes." Nate held out his hand. "Not sure which bank, but I can get my guys on it."

"That would be great."

"I can make copies of the book for each of us if that's okay with you?" Madison asked.

"Yes. I'd appreciate the help."

"I'll get it back to you tomorrow."

"I'd hoped to find some help." Claire's voice broke. "But I never dreamed I'd be this lucky."

"We're glad to help." Madison placed a hand on her arm. What Claire called luck, Madison saw as a blessing. And she was honored to be that blessing in her life. "I have some questions I'd like to ask you."

"Okay."

"Your brother talked about his three friends from the police force. Do you know their names and where they are today?"

"I can't remember their names right off, and I have no idea where they are now. Alan didn't keep in touch with them that I know of."

Madison glanced at Nate. This seemed so odd, but she didn't want to upset Claire any further. "If you remember or find their names, they could be useful. Maybe he decided to get in touch. Or one of them called him."

"I'll look through his things again. There's a photograph of the group. Maybe the names are on the back."

"I think that's all we can do for now." Nate pushed his chair away from the table. "We'll check back tomorrow. One more thing. Bring your brother's toothbrush and hairbrush by the station so we'll have samples of his DNA just in case."

"Okay." Claire paled.

"Try not to worry." He pressed his palms against the table and stood. "We'll find Alan."

A shudder ran down Madison's spine. Nate was careful not to say they'd find Alan alive. After all his years on the force, he knew better than to make false promises.

"WAIT UP." Rafe bolted out the front door and caught up with Claire. "I'll walk you home." He wouldn't pass up a chance to find out why she'd walked out on him all those years ago. He needed answers.

"No need." Claire flipped her hood up and secured it around her head.

"I should check the house before you go in."

"I can check it myself." Her tone was as icy as the wind. "Things have changed since we last saw each other."

"That's obvious." He allowed his hurt and frustration to color his words and immediately regretted it. "Forget I said that. It's late, and I'm tired."

She tramped away through the snow.

He stomped after her and reached a hand to touch her shoulder but pulled back. "I'm sorry, Claire. Seeing you again was a shock." He got in front of her, and she stopped. "I've missed you."

She raised her head, and moonlight sparked off her green eyes. "You didn't miss me that much, or you would have called. A girl can only wait so long." She stepped around him and walked off.

What did she mean he didn't call her? She'd written him a note telling him she wanted to end their relationship. Anger overwhelmed his self-control. "You're the one who broke up with me. Remember? You said you never wanted to hear from me again." He marched to his car, slammed the door, and drove off with what he intended to be a squeal of tires but ended up being a slip slide in the mushy snow.

At the top of the hill, he pulled to the curb and closed his eyes. No other woman in his life could get to him like Claire. But she was right. Things had changed since they were together. He'd changed. Gone was the wild boy who responded with his fists at the drop of a hat.

He'd like to think he'd become a man who thought things through, who could forgive, and who had his temper under control. With help from the Man Upstairs.

If that was true, how should he handle Claire's reappearance? The answer came to him from a place no MRI would ever find. He needed to put the past behind him and concentrate on helping her now. Whether she wanted him to or not.

He put his car in gear and drove back down the hill. He'd do what he did best. Find a place where he could keep an eye on the rental and make sure whoever messed with Alan didn't try anything with Claire. Good thing he'd filled the gas tank and thrown a blanket in the back.

After three hours, he found himself dozing off. Staying awake during an overnight surveillance in cold weather was more difficult than in the heat. He woke with a start and surveyed the surroundings. A shadow moved at the corner of the house. Rafe pulled a black balaclava over his head, grabbed his gun and flashlight, and eased out of the car.

The shadow disappeared around the corner. Rafe raced up the driveway and alongside the garage. He peered around the house. A man hunched over the lock on the sliding glass door. Rafe rounded the corner and took the deck stairs two at a time. "Put your hands in the air."

Instead of following instructions, the man rushed him, shoulder down, like a defensive end rushing a passer. He caught Rafe in the side and spun him around. As the man bounded down the steps, Rafe planted his feet. He blinked once and took aim.

The door opened behind him. "Get back in—" Something hard hit him on the back of the head, and he dropped to his knees. Pain ricocheted around inside his skull. The ski mask was torn from his face.

"Rafe."

A woman's voice sent fresh arrows of pain shooting through his brain.

"What are you doing here? I could have killed you."

"Get my gun." The statement came out in a low, slow voice. "You can finish the job."

"Very funny." She yanked on his arm. "Get inside, you big lug, and let me look at your head."

He staggered to his feet and stumbled. Claire supported him through the door and sat him on the edge of the recliner.

"Let me get a towel." She hurried away and returned a

moment later with a bath towel, which she used to cover the back of the chair. "There. Now you can lean back."

He tried, but the pain and dizziness were worse, so he stayed forward. "What's it look like?"

"Let me clean it off." Claire brought a basin of lukewarm, soapy water. The metallic scent of blood mixed with sweat wafted from where she parted his hair. "Ugh." She dabbed the injury with a warm, wet cloth.

"Ugh?"

"It's okay."

"Ugh doesn't sound okay."

"Well, you might need a couple of stitches?"

"Can you do them?"

"I don't have any sutures, and I haven't done stitches for a long time. If I can find some thread, I'll try if you want me to. Or I can take you to the hospital."

"No hospital." He hated them. "Call Madison. See if she has the stuff to do it."

"It's the middle of the night."

"So?"

"How about you call her?"

"Fine." He pushed a few numbers on his keypad.

"Rafe?" Madison's anxious voice answered after a couple of rings. "What's going on? Are you okay?"

"Do you have a suture kit? I'm next door, and I need stitches." He glanced at Claire.

"Stitches?" Nate's voice echoed in the background.

"I think I might. I'll be right over." Madison hung up before he could say more.

Rafe laid his phone aside. "Is it still bleeding?"

"No." Claire leaned close to examine his wound once more.

Memories of holding her washed over him. He brought her hand to his mouth and pressed a soft kiss to her palm. She shuddered and left it there a moment before pulling away.

"I need to empty this." When she lifted the pan of bloody water, her hands were trembling.

As he watched Claire walk into the kitchen, Rafe knew two things for sure. He wanted to renew a relationship with her, and it wasn't going to be easy.

He cleared his throat. "Get my gun. Please. It's on the deck."

"I know. I saw it when I helped you inside." She slipped into her parka and went through the slider. After five minutes, she returned, a look of alarm on her face. "It's not there."

A fist of unease settled in his stomach.

5

"What happened out there before I hit you?" Claire gestured at Rafe's head. A sudden chill skittered over her skin.

"I caught a guy sneaking around your house." Rafe ran a hand over his head and winced. "I was aiming at him when you clobbered me with—what did you hit me with anyway?"

"This." She pulled her pistol from her waistband. "At the last minute, I realized it was you and didn't hit you full force. You could be in a lot worse pain."

"Let me see it." He caught her hard stare. "Please."

Claire handed him the gun. "Does this meet with your approval, boss?

"Sorry. I didn't mean to—"

"It's okay." She waved his apology away. "I understand."

"This looks like government issue." He eyed her as he hefted her pistol.

"I'm an analyst with Homeland Security."

"A heavy gun for a woman to carry. Do you have a personal?"

"Not with me. I didn't plan on needing this one, but policy requires I have my weapon with me at all times." She sighed. "I'll

25

need to call my real boss in the morning and request more time off."

The doorbell rang, and Rafe returned her gun. "See who it is before you answer."

She gritted her teeth. "I know what to do." Keeping to one side of the hall, she approached the door, her gun at her side. "Who's there?"

"Madison. Open up. It's freezing."

Claire put her eye to the peephole. Madison stood shivering on the porch. The agent let their visitor in and did a quick scan of the street. Quiet. She secured the door with a snap of the bolt and followed Madison into the family room.

"It's about time," Rafe said. "I could have bled to death."

"You know," Madison paused with her coat halfway off and glared at him. "I can always leave and take my sutures with me."

"Rafe, that wasn't very nice." Claire stiffened. What had happened to him? When she'd known him before, he could be hard to get along with at times, but he was always kind to his friends.

"I'm sorry." Madison chuckled. "I forget that everybody's not used to how we banter back and forth." She grinned at Rafe.

"Madison's like the sister I never had." Rafe matched her grin with one of his own. "And I thank God for her every day."

An ache throbbed in Claire's chest as she set her gun on the side table. "I get it. Alan and I ..."

"I'm so sorry." Madison touched her arm. "We weren't thinking."

"I'm fine." Claire waved them off like she had before. "It's Rafe who needs your help."

"Show me where you need the stitches." Madison moved to the chair, all business now.

He bent his head and parted his hair.

"Ouch. What happened?"

He glanced at Claire and opened his mouth to speak.

"I hit him with the butt of my gun," she said.

Madison's eyes widened, and she pressed her fingers to her lips. "May I ask why?"

"I heard a noise on the deck, and when I went to investigate, I saw a man dressed in black with his back to me like he was running away." Claire shrugged. "So I hit him."

Madison shook her head at Rafe. "You're lucky she's not trigger-happy, or stitches would be the least of your worries."

"Can we get this over with? I feel like somebody's stomping on the back of my eyeballs." He rubbed his forehead between his eyes. "I need a handful of aspirin and a few days' sleep."

"Let's take him to Alan's room. He can stretch out on his side so you can see what you're doing." Claire hesitated about offering her brother's bed, but his was the only one on the first floor. No way could she and Madison get Rafe up the stairs. If Alan came home, he could use the other guest room on the second floor. The professional in her reasoned that her brother probably wouldn't be coming home, but the loving sister part of her continued to blow on an ember of hope.

Claire and Madison each reached for an arm, but Rafe shook them off. "I can walk on my own." After two steps, he lost his balance and almost fell into the fireplace.

"Easy now." Claire came alongside him and draped his arm over her shoulder. The warmth of his body seeped through the layers of clothes between them, and the attraction she once felt surged inside. She pushed it aside.

Madison supported him on his left, and they made it to the bedroom, where he fell onto the bed. Rafe closed his eyes and fell into a deep sleep. He didn't move at the sharp stick of the needle as his friend sewed him up.

"Will you be all right here tonight by yourself?" Madison asked. "I can send Nate over to sleep on the couch."

"We'll be fine. I'll sleep in the recliner again." Claire felt a twinge in her back. "Or maybe the couch. Besides, there's not much left of the night."

"True." Madison zipped her parka and pulled on her gloves.

"I'll leave the first aid kit with you. Call if you need anything. Keep an eye on him. I'm concerned about a concussion."

"I will. Thanks for taking care of him."

"Like he said, he's like a brother to me. How could I not come? Hopefully, we'll get some news about Alan tomorrow."

Claire nodded. The events of the day broke through the wall of her resolve, and she knew if she uttered another word, she'd end up in an ugly cry. Something she did not want to do in front of a woman she'd just met.

She secured the front door once more and slid to the floor, drawing her knees to her chest. A simple visit to her brother had turned into a nightmare. She could handle predicting how many casualties an incident might produce because they were numbers on a page. No problem. But up close and personal like this ripped her apart.

Her brother's disappearance was bad enough, but to be confronted with Rafe after all these years. She gazed at the bedroom door. Worry and confusion mixed with memories of past love tumbled around in her stomach while her brain screamed at her to focus on finding Alan.

And that was what she must do. She worked best with an objective. Pushing to her feet, she grabbed her gun from the living room and went in search of the photo of her brother and his friends on the police force. The frame hadn't been dusted in years. Four men in uniform. They smiled for the camera like they didn't have a care in the world. She worked the back off the frame, removed a folded piece of paper, and the photo.

Four names were written in her brother's spidery script on the back of the photo. Claire unfolded the paper and smoothed it out on the table. Again, she recognized her brother's handwriting, and as she read the first line, every nerve in her body shuddered.

Dear Claire,

If you're reading this, it means two things. One, I'm either dead or missing, and two, you suspect one of my "buddies" is involved.

It's a long story, but I can guarantee you're on the right path. Search for the key to my safe deposit box. You'll find the evidence you need in there.

I'm proud of you, sis. I hope after you learn the full story, you can forgive me and still love me.

Love, Alan

Alan knew he was in danger. That's why he'd asked her to come. And if she'd gotten here sooner, he might be ... She swallowed. No sense going there.

Now, she had to discover which bank held his safe deposit box and how she could gain access. As usual, her brother failed to give her all the facts. "I need more information, Alan." She shook the paper.

"What kind of information?" A man's voice sounded behind her.

6

Claire snatched her gun from where she'd set it on the table and spun around, adrenaline shooting through her.

"Whoa." Rafe backed against the refrigerator with both hands in the air.

"That's the second time I've almost killed you." She lowered her weapon. "You've got to stop sneaking around."

"I called from the doorway, but you didn't hear me. What are you doing?"

"I was looking at the photo of my brother and his police buddies." She took in his matted brownish-blond hair and pale face. "You don't look so good. Let me help you back to bed, and I'll get you some water."

"I'll go back to the recliner." He inclined his head toward the family room. "With a pillow."

She reached for his arm, but he waved her off.

"I can get there on my own if you'll take care of the rest."

She brought a pillow from the bedroom and positioned the cushion behind his head. As he laid back, he looked at her, and something caught in her chest. She'd forgotten that killer smile.

"I'll get you a bottled water. Do you want something to eat?"

"""

"No." He rocked his head back and forth. "Tell me what you found behind the photo."

"It's late, and I haven't slept at all." She yawned. "I need a couple hours, and then we'll talk."

"Leave your gun with me."

Giving someone else her service weapon was against protocol, but under the circumstances ... She gazed at him for a long moment before handing him her pistol. "I'll see you in a few hours."

She retrieved the photo and letter before climbing the stairs to her bedroom. Alan had prepared for her visit there too. The comforter and sheets appeared new and fresh. A storm of emotions brewed inside her, and despite the late hour and comfortable bed, she doubted she'd be able to do more than doze. But she was wrong.

The aroma of frying bacon and fresh coffee pulled Claire from a deep sleep. Her brain took a moment to catch up to her stomach. Her brother was cooking breakfast. No, not Alan. A tug at her heart brought her fully awake.

If Alan wasn't making breakfast, that meant it must be Rafe. He must be feeling a lot better. She showered and changed into fresh clothes before heading downstairs to join him. As she rounded the corner into the kitchen, she inhaled sharply.

"Good. You're up." Rafe turned from the stove and smiled. "Breakfast is ready."

He'd slicked his hair back, still damp from a shower, but his T-shirt caused her to stare. Alan's favorite. The one he'd bought when they visited the Grand Canyon two years ago.

Rafe noticed her gaze. "I'm sorry, Claire. I needed a clean shirt." He began to peel it off. "I should have asked first."

"No." She raised her hand to stop him. "It took me by surprise. That's all."

"You sure?"

"Yeah." She gave him a small smile and pulled a chair out at the table. "I'm starving. Where's that breakfast you promised?"

Rafe set a plate of bacon and eggs in front of her. "You still drink your coffee black?"

"I drink tea now."

"Coming right up."

Old memories of shared meals flooded her mind. She glanced at Rafe and was surprised to see his head bowed. When he raised his gaze to hers, she saw something there that tugged at her in a way she hadn't experienced before.

After Rafe finished his last bite, he pushed his plate to one side. "Time to talk about what you found with the photograph."

"I'll be right back."

When she returned, he'd cleaned up the dishes and moved to the dining room table. The curtains were open to another brilliant view of the lake. She laid the photo in front of him. "When Alan was on the force, these men were like brothers to him."

"He's a great guy. So was your other brother, David." Rafe studied the image.

Claire nodded. Scenes flashed in her mind of her younger brother, David, like snippets of video. She'd prayed so hard, but it didn't make any difference, and she wasn't in the mood to talk about David right now.

"Do you know who the other guys in the photo are?"

"He wrote their names on the back." Claire flipped the photo over.

"Does this say Dan or Don?"

"I think it's Don." Claire leaned closer. The woodsy scent of his soap tickled her nose.

"Your brother worked out of Chicago, right?"

"Yes."

"Jeannie may know these guys."

"Who's Jeannie?"

"Detective Jeannie Jansen. Works for Nate." He rose. "Come on."

"Chicago's a big place, Rafe." She shook her head. "I wouldn't count on her being of any help."

"You got a better idea?" He cocked an eyebrow at her.

She didn't, and he knew it. "Let me get my coat."

The drive to the police station took about twenty minutes, but it seemed much longer to Claire. Every nerve in her body buzzed with awareness of the man next to her. She'd never loved anyone like she'd loved him—before or after they were together. Now, here they were, and the feelings she thought she'd dealt with a long time ago were rising to the surface once more. She couldn't lose control. Not when her brother needed her at her sharpest.

As they approached the building, Rafe slowed his pace. "I need to warn you. Jeannie's different. She speaks her mind. You know where you stand with her." He shrugged.

"Kind of like you. Honest, but abrasive." Claire fixed him with an innocent stare.

"Yeah." He answered with a questioning frown. "I guess."

"I think I'll be okay." She patted his shoulder.

When they entered the police station, a petite woman with a blond ponytail marched toward them. She stopped in front of Claire. "So, you're the one who broke Rafe's heart."

"Yes, I am." Claire held out her hand. "And you're the one Rafe calls abrasive but honest."

Jeannie stiffened and glared at Rafe. Then she laughed and grabbed Claire in a bear hug. "He was a fool to let you get away."

Claire smiled into the woman's shoulder. "I agree."

"Now that you two have bonded, can we get down to business?" Rafe growled.

"Come on back. I already signed you in." Jeannie released Claire and led the way to her desk. "I understand your brother was a cop in Chicago."

"He was. For over twenty-five years. He quit five years ago and moved here last year."

"Why did he quit?"

"He wouldn't say." Claire had asked him that same question many times, but he refused to talk about it. "He told me he had his reasons, and they weren't any of my business."

"Let me see the photograph." Jeannie tapped her finger on the big man to the left of Alan. "Him, I know. Eugene Begay. I worked with him for a short time. Trouble wherever he went."

"What kind of trouble?" Rafe sat forward with his elbows on his knees.

"Small stuff. Roughing up suspects, suspicion of planting evidence, throwing his weight around." She leaned back. "Nothing that would stick in a court of law and nobody willing to testify against him. If you know what I mean."

"Do you recognize any of the others?"

She gave her head a slow shake. "This guy looks vaguely familiar." She pointed to Alan.

"That's my brother. You've probably seen him around town."

"That must be it." Jeannie waved the photo in the air. "Let me make a copy of this and do some checking. I still have friends on the force in the windy city."

"Great. I'd appreciate it."

Jeannie peered at the photo again. "This guy's kind of familiar too." She tapped the image of the man on the other end. "What's his name? Tommy Smith?" She shook her head. "Doesn't ring any bells." She left the room.

Maybe Alan had simply gone to visit one of his friends and forgotten about her visit. But why write that letter? No, for whatever reason, the three men in the photo had switched from being her brother's closest friends to being his worst enemies. If he was with one of them, it wasn't for a friendly visit.

7

"I appreciate your help." Claire put the photo back in her bag. "I know you've got better things to do than track down a few men who may or may not be connected with a man who may or may not be missing."

"Rafe wouldn't have brought you here if he didn't believe you." Jeannie furrowed her brow at the photocopy. "That's good enough for me."

"Here are the items Captain Zuberi asked for last night." Claire handed Jeannie the plastic baggies containing her brother's toothbrush and hairbrush.

"Detective Jansen." An officer approached the desk. "We received a call from a guy at the hardware store. Mathis Thoms is missing, and the place is a mess."

"Send somebody over to ... on second thought, I'll handle it. Send a forensics team." She jumped up.

Claire swallowed her frustration. The search for her brother would have to wait.

A TWINGE of disappointment poked Madison as she read the text from Rafe. She missed the days when she played a more active role in their cases. But she could still be useful. If she could decipher Alan's journal, it might provide answers to some of the questions about whether he was in touch with his old friends or not.

Photocopied pages of the battered book lay on the table next to her recliner. Along with a large glass of iced tea and a baggie of mixed nuts. As she settled in, the corners of her mouth lifted. She'd always loved puzzles.

The process seemed simple enough. She'd start with a word she was sure of and use those letters to interpret other words. Or at least make reasonable guesses. However, Alan's shorthand for names and places would take more thought. Madison scribbled notes in the margins and between the lines.

After a time, Oscar planted his front paws on her armrest and stuck his nose in her face.

"Hey." She pushed him down. "You know you're not supposed to get on the furniture."

He woofed at her and walked to the back door.

"I'm sorry. I wasn't paying attention." Madison leveraged herself out of her recliner and stretched. She opened the kitchen and porch door for Oscar. He raced out, took care of business, and then began his game with the snow. "Silly dog." His joyful antics warmed her heart.

As she turned to go back inside, Oscar stiffened, and his lips drew back in a snarl. His eyes locked on something to her left. Madison stepped into the kitchen to get a better view of the rental house next door.

A big man stood on the back deck. He yanked on the handle of the sliding glass door, but it didn't open. She grabbed her phone and slipped into her jacket and boots. The man caught sight of her as she trudged across the lawn toward Oscar.

"Can I help you?" She crossed her arms, holding her phone in a casual stance. She hit Video.

"Just looking for an old friend." The man stuffed his right hand in his jeans pocket and ran his left down his thick beard.

"I haven't seen the guy who lives there for days."

Oscar let out a low growl.

"If you want, I can take a message." Madison placed a hand on her black lab's head.

"Nah. That's okay. Just passing through. Thought I'd give it a try." The man gestured over his shoulder. "I need to be moving on." He turned his back to her and walked away.

As soon as he rounded the corner of the rental, Madison raced back inside. Oscar followed on her heels. She'd need to write down a description of the man, but first, she wanted to record his car as he left. With any luck, she'd get his license plate.

Their Christmas tree stood in the middle of the large window in her front room, with chairs flanking either side. She knelt in the chair to the right. Oscar woofed a second before she heard the crunch of his boots on the snow. Her breath snagged on the sudden fear inside her chest.

The man didn't drive away. He was almost to her front door.

Madison slid from the chair and crawled into the corner behind the curtains. She motioned for Oscar to join her. When he did, she wrapped her arms around him and her hands around his muzzle. "Not a sound," she whispered in his ear.

The doorbell rang. Oscar wiggled, and she tightened her grasp. A loud knock.

"Ma'am? I think I will leave a message."

Silence.

Bang. Bang. Bang. "Lady. I've changed my mind."

Madison peeked around the edge of the curtain. The man cupped his hands to the window and peered in. Oscar wrenched himself free and, for the second time that day, disobeyed the furniture rule. He leaped onto the chair directly in front of the man and pressed his evil-looking canines against the glass with a growl that rumbled deep in his chest.

The man stumbled back and caught himself before falling off the porch. He punched the glass, uttered a curse, and stomped off.

Madison drew her knees to her chest and waited for the shakes from the adrenaline let-down to pass. Maybe she didn't regret not playing a more active role after all. That was scary.

Then she remembered something even more frightening. She hadn't locked the back door.

8

As Rafe read the text from Madison, rough edges of unease pricked his soul. Had she run into the same guy he did the other night? If so, the man was gutsier than Rafe thought. And more unpredictable.

"We need to go." He rose and motioned to Claire. They followed Jeannie outside the police station.

"What's up?" Jeannie asked.

"Some guy was snooping around the house. Again."

"I'll let you know what I find out about Alan's friends and about Thoms." Jeannie strode to a black SUV and glanced over her shoulder.

"Thanks." He dipped his head. "Talk soon."

With a brisk wave, Jeannie got into her vehicle and roared away.

Back in his car, Rafe handed Claire his phone, opened to the text from Madison. "You better read this."

"Oh, no. Now that she's got a look at him, she could be in danger too."

"Yeah." He pressed his lips together in suppressed frustration. "In the beginning, I didn't understand why Nate would get so angry with me whenever she ended up in a

41

dangerous situation. It was her job. If she didn't want to do it, she could quit. But now ..." He banged the steering wheel with his hand. "Now I get it. She's like a sister to me."

"You could fire her."

"I've tried. But she won't let me. She loves the work and says she should be able to do what she wants." He cut his eyes to Claire. "You should understand that."

"I do."

"Since the twins, she's confined her role to the laboratory and research." He pulled into the driveway. "Until today."

Madison opened the door before they could ring the bell.

"How do you do that?" Claire asked.

"My advanced warning system." Madison nodded to where Rafe rubbed Oscar's head. "He lets me know when anyone is coming to the door, and I can tell whether it's someone I know by his tail."

"Is that how you knew the man snooping around my brother's rental was on your front porch?"

"Yes and no." Madison led the way into the kitchen. "Can I get you something to drink?"

"Coffee." Rafe pulled a chair out for Claire.

"Do you have any tea?"

"I have iced tea or bags to make hot tea."

"Iced tea is good."

"Tell me what happened. From the beginning." Rafe took the mug of coffee and thanked her.

"I can do better than that." Madison opened her laptop and pulled up a video. "The footage isn't the best. I had my arms crossed, trying to act casual, and I was freezing."

An image of a man standing on the deck of the rental appeared on the screen. The picture was clear but tilted to the right. Rafe paused the video. Tall, with a full dark beard and mustache. A knit cap pulled down over his ears showed no hair around the edges, and mirrored sunglasses hid his eyes. Rafe pressed Play.

Madison's voice sounded, asking if she could help. The man's answer was faint. Rafe turned up the volume. Deep voice with no discernible accent.

"As soon as he was out of sight, I went back inside. My idea was to get video of his car." Madison took a drink of tea. "He almost caught me in the act. Oscar woofed like he does, and when I heard the man's boots on the snow, I couldn't believe it. I hid behind the curtain."

"What were you thinking?" Rafe glared. "You shouldn't have confronted the guy in the first place. That's what nine-one-one is for."

"I wasn't thinking." She shot a piercing look back at him. "I guess I'm not as perfect as you are."

"Rafe, cool it." Claire raised her hands. "Madison's been through enough today."

He strode to the kitchen window and waited for his irritation to subside. What could they learn from this? He pulled out a chair. "Did he touch anything? The slider next door? Your doorknob?"

"He had gloves on the whole time." Madison straightened. "But he would have left boot prints in the snow. If that helps."

"Better than nothing." He ran a hand down his face. "I called Jeannie. She and a team will be over after they finish at the Thoms crime scene, and she has a talk with his wife."

"I imagine Nate knows what happened." She fingered the silver cross at her neck.

"Yes." He averted his gaze from her anxious face. Madison would catch grief from her police captain husband too.

Oscar walked to the back door and looked at them.

"I'll take him." Rafe pulled on his coat and gloves. He ruffled the big dog's head. "You want to go out and play in the snow?"

CLAIRE WATCHED THEM GO. "He loves that dog."

"And Oscar loves him." Madison gave a dry laugh. "Sometimes, I think more than me."

"I doubt that." She turned. "If it's any consolation, I would have done the same thing you did."

Madison gave her a brief smile. "Thanks, but I don't think Rafe or my husband would agree with you."

"What do men know about it." She rolled her eyes. "They still think we're the weaker sex."

She and Madison shared a chuckle.

"Besides, how could you know the guy would react like he did? You thought he'd left. I would have too." Claire pointed to Madison's phone. "At least you got him on video, which is a big deal. Send that to me and Rafe so we have copies."

"I will." Madison picked up her phone. The doorbell chimed. "That must be Jeannie." She left and returned with the detective.

"The team is looking around outside." Jeannie poured herself a cup of coffee. "Where's Rafe?"

"Out back with Oscar."

"Figures." The detective walked to the kitchen window. "He can be such a kid sometimes."

"Claire suggested I send a copy of the video I made of the intruder to her and Rafe."

"Send one to me too." Jeannie marched over to her. "Did you recognize the guy?"

"No."

"Why?" Claire directed her question to Jeannie. "Does his description sound familiar?"

"Give me a minute to check it out." Jeannie sat at the table and opened the file on her phone.

Claire tensed as she studied Jeannie's face. If the detective knew the intruder, they'd be one step closer to finding her brother. After a moment, Jeannie shook her head.

"He sounded a lot like Mathis Thoms." Jeannie rubbed her eyes with her thumbs. "But it's not. After what we found at his store, I can't imagine he's still alive."

"Is that how you feel about Alan too?" Despair swept through her like a cold wind.

Jeannie twisted the cup in her hand. "We found blood at the hardware store. Lots of it." She gave Claire a tired look.

"We have no reason to believe Alan is dead." Madison placed a hand on Claire's arm.

She looked at the woman next to her. Something about Madison made her feel at peace.

"She's right." Jeannie took out her notebook. "You said there weren't any signs of a struggle in the house and no blood. It's more likely he's in hiding. Running from someone."

"Why wouldn't Alan contact me if that were the case?" That explanation didn't make sense.

"I don't know, but I do have more information on his friends from the police force." Jeannie squinted at her notes. "At least two of them. I haven't been able to find anything on Tommy Smith."

The kitchen door opened, and Oscar made a beeline for Jeannie.

"Hi, buddy." She ruffled his ears before returning her attention to her notes. "What was I saying?" She held the papers away from her and squinted.

"Here. Try using these." Rafe handed Jeannie a pair of glasses sitting on the table close by. "You haven't found anything on Tommy Smith."

She grunted her thanks. "As for the Indian Chief, Eugene Begay, he's gone legit. Sort of. He owns a fabrication company that's in line for a government contract. The scuttlebutt in the business world is that he's slick, but nobody would give me details." She lifted her mug in Madison's direction. "Could I have a refill?"

"Sure." Madison poured Jeannie a fresh cup and sat next to her.

"Don Irving is about to become very well known. He's running for U.S. Representative from Ohio. He started as a councilman in Cleveland and made a quick rise from there. Too quick if you ask some people." She took a sip. "I'm trying to get financials on all of them, but as you can imagine, without much cause, it's tough."

"Why did you call Begay, Indian Chief?" Claire asked.

"Every beat cop in Chicago has a nickname. Begay is part Navajo, so his was Indian Chief." Jeannie shrugged.

"What was yours?" Rafe asked.

A flush climbed up Jeannie's neck. "Never mind." Her phone buzzed, and she furrowed her brow.

"What?"

"A body. I have to go."

9

Blood pounded in Claire's ears. "I'll go with you." She jumped up. "It might be Alan."

"I'm sorry. You can't. I'll let you know as soon as I do." Jeannie hurried out of the kitchen.

Claire heard the door slam. She grabbed Rafe by the shirt. "You have to find out where the body is and take me there."

"I can't. It's police business." He encircled her with his arms. "Please, Claire, Jeannie's a good cop."

She pushed him away and yanked on her coat and boots. "I'm going back to the rental."

"Claire, please stay." Madison caught her eye in a pleading look.

She hesitated. Why did this woman have such an effect on her? She forced herself to turn away. "I'll be back later." She needed time to think. Time to plot her own course of action.

Once inside the condo, she'd half expected Rafe to follow and listened for a knock at the door, but none came. Was he respecting her space, or did he think she was pouting? And why did it matter?

She picked up her brother's journal and settled into his recliner again. This time, she turned to the last page. It was dated five days ago. She could decipher one entry and read it aloud. "*C* here in three days." The other entries made no sense.

P with a check mark. *IC* with a check mark. Was that Indian Chief? When she thumbed back through the diary, she found the identical notations at regular intervals. Only earlier ones included *L* with a check mark too. She started making notes about the dates, when her phone vibrated on the table beside her.

Her heart lurched in her chest. "Claire Green."

"Jeannie wants us at the station." Rafe's sober tone chilled her. "I'll pick you up."

Alan was dead. What else could it be? She stood and took three deep breaths before pulling on her parka and boots.

They rode to the station house in silence. She was thankful Rafe didn't try to comfort her with empty platitudes.

At the police station, Jeannie led them back to her desk. "Sit." She indicated two chairs and looked at Claire. "First, the body isn't your brother."

Claire stared at her. Had she heard right? Alan wasn't dead? Then why—

"It's Mathis Thoms." Jeannie opened a file in front of her. "The reason I called you two down here is because he was shot with your gun." She nodded at Rafe.

"You found my gun at the scene?"

"No, but the markings on the bullets that killed Thoms match those we have on file."

"Why do they have a file on your gun?" Claire turned a questioning look on Rafe.

"I was involved in a firefight last year." He rubbed the bridge of his nose.

Claire returned her attention to Jeannie. "If the dead man's not my brother, why did you need me here?"

"We found a strand of your brother's hair on the body."

One of Alan's hairs on Mathis Thoms? The professional part of her brain ran through what Jeannie had said and came up with a conclusion her heart didn't like at all. "You think Alan was my intruder last night, stole Rafe's gun, and shot Mathis Thoms?" She threw her arms in the air. "That makes no sense. What was his motive, and why would he break into a house he has the key to?"

"Maybe he lost his keys or left them behind?" Jeannie didn't break eye contact with Claire.

"I haven't found any keys in the house." Claire sat back and wrapped her arms around her waist.

"Lost them then."

"How do you know it's one of Alan's hairs?"

"We collected samples from his brush. Remember?"

Of course. "But why would he kill Thoms?

"I don't have the answer yet, but I will."

Anger built in Claire like a dry pine tree catching fire. She stood and pressed her palms on Jeannie's desk. "My brother isn't like that. I don't care what the evidence says. He didn't do it."

"I didn't say he did." Jeannie rose too. "But I'm a police officer, and I must consider all possibilities. As a professional, you should understand that."

She had a point, but this was Claire's brother. She found it hard to look at this from a professional point of view.

"Alan won't be the only one we investigate. We'll consider any and all possible suspects."

Claire stood an inch taller than the ponytailed detective, but Jeannie's commanding presence made up for the lack of height. Fighting with her was pointless. "I need to go. If you have anything more to tell me, I'll be at Alan's house."

She spun on her heel and headed for the exit. Before she remembered Rafe had driven her to the station. Nothing was going right for her that day.

"I'll take you back." He glanced at Jeannie, who nodded.

"I'm sorry, Claire. I'm just doing my job." Jeannie's voice reached her over the noise of the precinct.

She understood, but the day had left her feeling bruised and uncertain of what was true. Was her brother alive, and if so, did he kill Mathis Thoms?

Madison pressed End and set her phone on the table next to her. Mathis Thoms was dead, and Alan Green was the prime suspect. She ached for Claire. The poor woman had run the gamut from concern about her brother's disappearance to worry about his possible involvement in a murder in less than forty-eight hours.

Rafe had convinced Madison not to rush next door. He said Claire needed time alone, and Madison knew how that felt. For now, she'd do what she did best. Pray.

And research. She picked up Alan's journal once more. Shadows invaded the room as the sky grew dark. She flipped on the lamp by her side and glanced at her phone. Nate hadn't called. Was he mad about her confronting the strange man today? She paused with her finger hovering over Nate's name.

Oscar woofed, and the garage door rattled open. Her husband was home. Time to see for herself. She smoothed her blouse and prepared herself for whatever was to come.

Nate removed his coat and bent to rub Oscar behind the ears as usual. When he straightened, he gazed at her for a long moment before striding across the floor and wrapping her in his arms. Tears sprang unbidden to her eyes and soaked into his sports coat.

"I wanted to give you a lecture, but I remembered our agreement." He rubbed her back. "If you're expected to let me do my job even when it could be dangerous, I need to do the same. It's not easy for me, but I respect and trust you."

"In this instance, it wasn't the best decision. All I can say in my defense is I'm rusty. I haven't seen action for a while." She buried her face in his chest. "Thank God for Oscar."

"Yes." He held her for several minutes. "Thank God."

When he released her, he leaned back and wiped her cheeks with his thumbs. "I'll get changed, and we'll throw something together for dinner. Then you can tell me what's going on with the case."

She drew him in for a kiss. "I love you, Nate Zuberi."

"I love you more, Madison Zuberi." He patted her bottom. "Now fix me some food, woman."

Half an hour later, Madison related everything that happened that day and showed him the video as they ate.

"Alan is no killer." Nate shook his head. "Unless I've totally lost my ability to read people."

"That's how I feel too. But the evidence is pointing his way."

"A strand of hair is pretty circumstantial." Nate rinsed his plate and put it in the dishwasher. "I wonder if they have anything more."

"Jeannie didn't say."

"I'll talk to her tomorrow."

"By the way, did your guys ever find out what bank the safe deposit key belongs to?"

"Yes. Ross County Banking Center."

"Are there many branches?"

"Sixteen."

Madison sighed.

Nate slid his arm around her waist and pulled her to his side. "It's not as bad as it sounds. They may not all have safe deposit boxes. Even if they do, it's just a matter of finding out which one Alan Green used."

"And figuring out how Claire can gain access."

"She may not have to if her brother becomes a suspect in the Thoms murder. We'll be able to get into it for her."

"That's true." There was a bright side to everything.

"Send me the video, and I'll make sure the guy's face gets run through all the recognition software." He kissed her.

Oscar yipped and trotted over to the slider leading from the kitchen onto the porch.

"I'll take the big guy out while you clean up." Nate shrugged into his heavy coat and boots. "Come on, buddy, make it quick. No playing. I want time to relax with a *Law and Order* rerun before bed."

She laughed. "I can't believe you like that show."

"You got me hooked."

A chill breeze swept through the house as the dog and his master left. Madison placed the last bowl in the dishwasher and stepped from the kitchen onto the enclosed porch. The heater struggled to keep the space warm, and she shivered. Oscar explored the yard for any strange smells while Nate stood back against the house out of the wind. Her heart swelled with love for both man and dog.

Nate called to the dog, and Oscar turned to race back to the house. The crack of a rifle shot echoed off the frozen lake. Snow exploded where her precious pet had stood a split second ago.

10

Madison froze. Somebody shot at her dog. Nate grabbed Oscar by the collar and rushed through the door.

"Get down." He pushed her to the floor and yanked his phone from his jacket pocket. "Shots fired at Thirty-two Pleasant Valley Lake Drive."

The ding of a text reached Madison's ears. Her phone was on the kitchen table.

"Leave it. We need to stay put."

She hated lying on the floor in the dark. "What if the shooter is sneaking up on us?"

"I'll crawl into the kitchen and turn the lights off. You follow with Oscar."

Once inside, she went to the blue cupboard where she kept her gun and handed it to Nate. She hunkered on the floor, wrapped her arms around Oscar, and waited for the sirens and lights. It wasn't long before the familiar screaming of police cars broke the nighttime peace.

Nate met the officers at the door and led them to the kitchen, which was now brightly lit again. The aroma of brewing coffee filled the air. As she listened to Nate relate the incident to the police, it seemed surreal. Who would want to shoot at her dog?

She gazed at the peaceful scene outside her kitchen window. Moonlight reflected off glittering snow. All around the lake, Christmas lights twinkled on houses and in windows.

A cold chill skittered down her spine as she pictured the man with the beard and mustache. Could he have been the one who shot at Oscar? She turned from the window and picked up her phone.

The text was short. She handed her cell phone to Nate.

"What's this?"

"Read it."

"That was a warning." His eyes locked on hers. "Is this the text you got while we were on the porch?"

She nodded.

He rose and wrapped her in his arms. "We'll get this jerk. I won't let anything happen to you or Oscar."

"I love you." But she knew there were no guarantees when it came to bad guys.

Nate released her and showed the police officer the text.

"We'll leave a patrol car outside tonight and be back with a metal detector to find the bullet," one officer said.

"Thanks, guys." Nate walked them to the door. When he returned, he pulled her in another hug. "I think we've had enough drama for one day."

"Me too." She shuffled down the hall toward their bedroom. "I may sleep in my clothes tonight. I'm not sure I have the energy to change into my pajamas."

"That's okay." Nate grinned. "I'll help you."

"I'm sure you will." She intertwined her arm with his. "Let's go to bed."

"I thought you'd never ask."

Oscar plopped down in the bedroom doorway with a big sigh.

RAFE FINISHED his exercises and took a shower. Now, for breakfast with a good cup of coffee. As he entered the kitchen, his chin dropped to his chest. He enjoyed house-sitting for his Aunt Sarah and Uncle Ed except for one thing. They didn't drink coffee.

Good thing they lived next to Madison. She always had a pot brewing. He donned his boots and jacket and headed out.

A police car sat at the curb, and his walk turned into a jog. He burst through the front door without knocking, and for the first time, Oscar met him with barking and teeth bared.

"Whoa, boy. It's me." Rafe backed against the wall with his hands raised in a gesture of surrender.

The hair on the dog's back flattened, and he sidled up to Rafe, his whole body wagging as if asking forgiveness.

"You're a good boy." Rafe rubbed his neck. "Good watch dog. I shouldn't have barged in like that, huh?"

Madison and Nate stood in the room, gaping at him as if he'd lost his mind. "I saw the police car. It spooked me." He shrugged. "I haven't had my coffee."

"You'd better come in." Madison turned on her heel. "Who knows what you'll do next."

"Why is the panda car outside?" Rafe poured himself a cup of coffee.

"You didn't hear the shot last night?" Nate asked. "Or the sirens?"

"When?" Rafe pinned Nate with a glare. "Why didn't you call me?"

"About nine." Nate glared back. "And we were a little busy."

Rafe lowered his cup. "I fell asleep with my earbuds in. I woke up about eleven and went to bed."

"By then, all the action was over," Madison said over her shoulder.

"Someone shot at Oscar." Nate put a plate of eggs and bacon in front of him. "We think it was the same guy Madison caught snooping around the rental."

"What makes you think that?"

Madison showed him the text on her phone. A lump of cold hard anger formed in his throat. Nobody messed with his people. "I'll have my guys help with guard duty. If you want, I can get Zoe to stay with you until we get this dirtbag."

"Thanks. I'll let you know." Nate finished his coffee and put his mug in the sink. "For now, I'd appreciate a few of your men on watch around the neighborhood. You've got his photo."

"No problem." Rafe washed down his breakfast with another mug of caffeine. "I'll have my guys in place in an hour."

"Good. Some officers are coming out to recover the bullet sometime this morning. We'll touch base later." Nate gave Rafe a nod. "I appreciate your help."

"You're family. I'll do whatever you need." Rafe pushed his chair back and stood. "Have you heard from Claire? Did she come over last night when everything was happening?"

"No, she didn't." Madison shared a worried look with Nate. "I was so upset I didn't even think about her."

"She was probably asleep. I'll go check on her." Rafe slipped his jacket from the back of the chair.

"How was she when you left her yesterday?" Madison asked. "Do you want me to go with you?"

"No." He recalled the misery on Claire's beautiful face. "Hopefully, she's in a better place today." He gave his friend a brief smile and left the house. Every step turned into a mantra of prayer. *Give me the right words. Help me say the right thing. Show me when to speak and when to listen.* He rang the bell. No answer. Knocked. Nothing.

Unease crawled along his spine. Had the man who'd shot at Oscar gained entrance to the rental? He banged on the door. "Claire." He could open the door with his passkey, but if she was in the shower ...

He leaned on the bell several more times before slipping his key into the lock. He cracked the door open and listened. No sound of running water. "Claire? It's Rafe." No answer. "Are you in there?" He stepped inside. "Claire?"

He did a quick search of the house. She wasn't there.

11

Claire slid the back door open, knocked the snow off her boots, and stepped inside.

"Hi," a male voice said.

She yanked her gun from her waistband, crouched, and aimed in the direction of the voice. After being outside, the room was filled with shadows. She blinked in an attempt to acclimate her vision. Her hand remained rock steady despite the shaking she felt inside.

Rafe walked to the middle of the room with his hands up. "Sorry. I—"

"Do you have a death wish? That's three times I've almost killed you." Claire dropped into a chair at the dining table and placed her pistol on its smooth surface. "How did you get in here?"

"I have a key." He sat across from her. "I came over to check on you. When no one answered, I let myself in."

"You did what?" She cut her eyes to her gun. Tempting.

"I didn't sneak in. I announced myself, Agent Green." His glare was as hard as the edge in his voice. "I was worried about you."

She ran a finger along a vein in the oak tabletop. "I'm fine."

"Where were you?"

"Out back." She'd needed some fresh air away from all the reminders of Alan. "What's going on at Madison's house?"

"Someone shot at Oscar last night. You didn't hear it either?"

"No. Is he all right?" Poor Oscar. And Madison.

"Yeah. They're searching for the bullet with a metal detector."

Relief calmed her anxiety to a degree, but she knew since Madison could identify the man who was on her deck, she'd be a threat to him. Her friend was still in danger.

"What are you thinking?" Rafe narrowed his eyes at her.

"I'm trying to figure out what, if anything, I can do to help keep Madison safe."

"My men will be on guard around the neighborhood." He reached for her hand. "But she could always use your prayers."

"I don't believe in prayer anymore." Claire flashed him an angry look. "Not since we lost David."

"Your brother had a strong faith—"

"My brother suffered. It didn't matter how much I prayed. Or how strong his faith was." She wouldn't listen anymore. "And now Alan is gone too." She ran down the hall and up the stairs to her bedroom.

"Claire. Please." He called to her from the bottom of the staircase. "I'm going. Call if you need me."

A subtle change in pressure inside the house as he opened the door and closed it once more signaled he'd left. She came out of her bedroom and sat on the top step. The window above the front door offered a view of the neighborhood from a different perspective. That was exactly what she needed—a new perspective. But with everything spinning out of control, how could she get one?

RAFE GLANCED up as he left the rental and gave himself a mental head slap. How could he have forgotten about the cameras? He'd installed video surveillance of both the front and back of the rental home two years ago. He jogged back to his aunt and uncle's house with a possible lead in hand.

Rafe slouched on the couch, his computer on his lap. The camera footage for the rental from two months ago scrolled across his screen, and he checked all visitors with notations in Alan's journal. So far, he verified *B*'s visit on the twentieth of November.

Seemed normal. He was in and out within an hour. Didn't try to hide his face, but Rafe didn't recognize him.

Alan left town for Thanksgiving and returned the following Monday. No one approached the house during that time. Rafe rubbed the corners of his eyes and advanced the film. By the first week in December, the weather was consistently gray and blowing snow. Alan stayed inside.

Rafe sat up. A man appeared seemingly out of nowhere on Alan's front porch. He wore a long, hooded coat that obscured his face. The door opened, and Alan let him in. He stared at the screen, which showed shots of the front and back doors as the clock in the corner rolled through the minutes. What was going on in there?

He hovered his finger over the button to speed things along when the man followed Alan through the back door and disappeared into the darkness.

Sometime later, the man returned to the house.

"Look at the camera," Rafe muttered. "Just for a second."

But he didn't. He was inside when *B* showed up for his scheduled meeting. He rang the bell several times and knocked before finally giving up and walking away.

On the way to his car, he stopped and looked at something on the ground. He glanced back at the house before getting in his car and leaving. The other man stayed for another half hour before exiting through the front door.

Rafe closed his laptop and stood. When Rafe rented the house, he had no idea Claire was Alan's sister. Green was a common last name, so she hadn't even crossed his mind. Would that have made a difference? He rubbed the back of his neck. No, but it made it even harder to watch her brother get kidnapped. Or worse. He should look at the rest of the tapes, but he couldn't sit still any longer. He needed a good workout.

But first, he'd take a copy of the tapes to Jeannie. He plugged a memory stick into his computer and started the download.

"All stations check in." He keyed his walkie-talkie and shrugged into his coat.

"Two, check."

"Three, check."

"Number One?" One was stationed closest to the rental. His hand tightened on the communicator.

"One, check. Sorry for the delay."

"Base out. Use cell."

Three clicks answered.

12

Madison looked longingly out at one of the few sunny days they would get this month and yearned to put on her skates and hit the ice. The man who shot at Oscar wouldn't have stuck around—not with all the activity in the neighborhood today. She should be fine. At least for a short time.

She slipped onto the porch, making sure Oscar couldn't follow. "You need to stay inside, boy. I'm not taking any chances you'll get hurt."

The big dog whined with his nose pressed against the glass as she pulled on her ski pants and parka and threw her skates over her shoulder. "I won't be long." She gave him a little wave before trudging down the deck and across the lawn to the edge of the lake.

A light dusting of blowing snow covered the ice where she'd cleared it two days ago. She pushed off and glided around the semicircle, concentrating on how good it felt to stretch her muscles and feel the cold air on her face. It was so quiet. Too quiet. She missed the twins. Their chattering and giggles. Even their bickering.

A man slogged through the snow behind the rental in her direction. "Mrs. Zuberi?"

She shielded her eyes and prayed she hadn't made a big mistake as she peered at the approaching figure. One of Rafe's men. Her pulse slowed. "What is it?"

"I'm not sure it's a good idea for you to be out here like this." The man tramped to the edge of the ice about ten feet farther along the bank.

"Don't step out there." Madison held out her arms. "That's where one of the springs is located. The ice is thin. You'll fall through."

He backed up.

"Could I have another five minutes? I've been stuck inside for what seems like forever." She skated in a small circle.

"Five minutes." He moved her way along the bank. "Then I'll escort you back to your house."

"Thanks." She did as many circuits of her small rink as she could in that short period. Who knew when she'd be able to get out there again?

"You're good." He carried her skates back to the house. "How long you been skating?"

"Most of my life." She stepped inside and hung up her parka. "I grew up in St. Louis. My dad took me when I was a little girl. Would you like a cup of to-go coffee?"

"Yes, ma'am. That would be great."

One good thing about going back inside. Oscar greeted her like she'd been away a week. "I know, puppy, you hate staying inside as much as I do." She rubbed his head. "We'll have to see what we can do about that."

She handed the man his coffee in an insulated mug. "Thanks for watching out for us."

"No problem."

After pouring herself a cup of coffee, she picked up her copy of Alan's appointment book. She was making progress. According to her notes, Alan had three regular notations and two that showed up sporadically. One she suspected was Claire.

After the conversation with Jeannie, she was reasonably

certain the three recurring ones were Alan's friends from the force. *IC* was Indian Chief, Eugene Begay. Now, to work out the other two. How did that song go? "Rich man, poor man, beggarman, thief, doctor, lawyer, or Indian chief." Madison recited it aloud.

Was *L* lawyer? That might fit Don Irving since he ended up running for State Representative. Which meant Smith was *P*. Poor man? Possibly. Wonder what Alan's nickname was?

There was one more notation to figure out. Alan got sporadic visits from someone he called *B*. Beggarman? The last time was two days before Claire was due to arrive. Could this man have something to do with Alan's disappearance?

Oscar's ears perked up, and he woofed once. The rumble of the garage door echoed through the house. Nate? So early? Oscar rose and went to the door, his tail beating the air.

"Hi, big guy." Her handsome husband, his dark brown hair disheveled as always, bent to pet their dog.

A smile lifted the corners of her mouth.

"I thought I'd surprise you and get home early for a change." He checked his watch. "Or earlier, anyway."

"You surprised me all right. I haven't started supper yet." She put his coat on a chair and slid her arms around his neck. "But I am so glad to see you." She pulled his head down and pressed her lips to his.

After sharing a few more kisses, she rested her head on his chest and listened to his strong, comforting heartbeat.

"Madison?"

"Yes, sweetheart." She burrowed deeper into his warmth.

"Do I have time for a bath before supper?

She reared back and furrowed her brow. "That's it? No sweet nothings or endearments? Just 'do I have time for a bath?'"

"Well ... yes." His brown eyes twinkled with mischief.

"You are such a man." She laughed. "Go take your bath."

"Love you." He bent to kiss her again.

"Too late." She dodged him and grabbed Oscar by the collar. "I'll take Oscar out and then start your supper."

Outside, the sun was low on the horizon, and the temperatures were dropping into the freezing range once more. Madison was glad she'd taken the time to put on her ski pants and parka to come outside with her dog.

As she and Oscar headed back to the house, a man appeared around the corner of the rental. This time, Oscar didn't hesitate. He shot toward the intruder in a black blur, leaving Madison screaming after him.

The man raced for the lake. She yelled for him to stop, to no avail. He ran to the end of the rental's pier and jumped onto the ice. His left foot broke through, and he screamed for help.

Oscar stood on the end of the pier, barking.

"Stop," Madison ordered her dog and spoke to the man grappling for hold on the ice. "I'm coming out to you. Try to stay calm." She found the rope left on the dock and slipped the looped end over one of the poles.

As she edged her way out on her belly, the crack of the ice under his other leg sent more chills down her spine.

"Hurry. I'm going under." The fear in his voice urged her to move faster, but his best chance required her to keep her cool.

"Try to stay as still as possible. I'm almost there." She moved out and approached his head. "I have a rope. Can you grasp it?"

"I'm afraid to let go."

"Okay. I'll try to get close enough to get it around your body." She inched closer until she and the man were face to face. "Stay very still." *Help me, Lord.* She wormed the rope through a narrow space between his chest and the ice. The man's rapid breathing had the sour smell of fear.

The ice cracked once more, but the man maintained his position. She managed to catch the end of the rope and pull it across his back. With a quick twist of her wrists, she tied a knot. "Now to pull you out."

The ice gave under his other leg, and he slipped under the

water. Madison grabbed the rope and scurried as fast as she could toward the thicker ice behind her. She pulled with all her strength. The man's head and shoulders appeared above the water. He gasped and spat out the frigid lake water.

"Try clawing your way toward me while I pull." Her muscles ached, but she couldn't—wouldn't—let go.

Nate appeared on the ice beside her. He took the rope and pulled the man out onto his stomach.

"Aah. Stop." He coughed violently. "Something ... around ... ankle." He clasped the rope and panted.

"I'll get my hook." Madison ran for the house, praying Nate could hold the man and the ice underneath them didn't break.

When she returned, she slid once more to the edge of the hole where the man's legs dangled in the water. "Which foot is it?"

"Right." His teeth chattered, and his body shook.

Madison guided the hook along the frozen man's right leg until she felt an obstruction. Easing the hook around it, she searched for a hold. When she thought she'd found one, she lifted. "Can you move your leg now?"

He nodded.

"She pulled upward, hand over hand on the pole, while Nate helped the man out of the hole. When the man's foot appeared at the water's surface, she saw what was holding him. A ski rope. And it was tied to something heavy.

Nate got hold of the rope. "Let me see if I can get that out of there." He pulled on the rope. Something began to rise from the depths of the lake.

Madison put her face closer to the water. What was it? Something white and bloated. Another dead carp? With a surge, the object rose to the surface. The filmy white eyes of a body stared at her from pale, swollen features.

13

Madison scrambled back from the hole, her brain screaming *get away*. The only thing that stopped her was the sound of Nate's familiar deep voice.

"I'm going to secure the rope with the body in place and hope it holds long enough for someone from the ME's office to get here." He glanced at the man curled into a fetal position on the ice. "I need you to call nine-one-one and Rafe to get one of his men to help get this guy into the house before he freezes to death."

She'd forgotten about the intruder who'd fallen into the lake. In the waning light, his lips appeared almost black. She got to her feet and, with a purpose in hand, bolted for the shoreline, giving in to her desire to flee.

Oscar raced after her and, once inside, followed her into the kitchen, where she grabbed her phone.

"Nine-one-one. What's your emergency?"

"A man fell through the ice behind our house. We need an ambulance. Also, we discovered a body under the ice when we were getting him out. We need the medical examiner and homicide out here ASAP."

"What's your address?"

"Thirty-two Pleasant Valley Lake Drive. Captain Zuberi's home."

"I've alerted the ambulance and the other departments, Mrs. Zuberi."

"Thanks." Madison pressed End and punched in Rafe's number.

"What's going on?" Rafe's voice was edged with steely concern.

"Nate needs your help." She passed a shaky hand across her forehead. "A man fell through the ice behind the house, and we found a dead man under the ice."

"I'll be right there."

"Thanks." But she was talking to a dial tone.

What next? She stared out the kitchen window. Nate dragged the man toward shore. *Please, Lord, give Nate the strength he needs and keep them from going through the ice.*

The man would need dry clothes. She hurried to their bedroom and dug a pair of Nate's sweatpants and shirt from the chest of drawers. The easiest access to the house from the lake was through the basement door. They could put the stranger in the spare bedroom down there. Madison turned to Oscar. "Go to your rug."

The black lab slunk over to the rug by the door to the garage. He stood there a moment, looking at her with his dark eyes as if he wasn't sure why he was in trouble.

"Lay down. Stay." She'd love on him later, but for now, she needed him to stay out of the way.

He circled two times and plopped down with a heavy sigh.

She gathered some blankets and descended the stairs to the basement living area. A wall of windows looked out to the lake from the cozy recreation room. The doors to the spare bedroom and bath were located along the back wall.

Nate and Rafe carried the man up the slight incline toward the house. They made slow progress in the snow. Madison opened the basement door and grabbed a toboggan leaning against the wall. She slogged over to the men. "Will this help?"

"Good idea."

The men laid the stranger on the sled and pulled him across the snow to the downstairs patio.

Once everyone was inside, Madison directed them to the spare bedroom where she'd left Nate's clothes. "Take off his wet ones and put on the ones I left on the bed. Get him covered in blankets. Let me know what else you need."

"Great." Nate shrugged out of his parka and handed it to her. "Make some hot tea with lots of sugar."

"Will do." She took the steps two at a time, tossed Nate's jacket on a chair, and filled her electric kettle with water.

Oscar sat up and barked once. She ran to the front window. Flashing red and blue lights reflected off the houses as the emergency vehicles sped down the hill. Not the kind of lights anyone likes to see in their neighborhood at Christmas.

When the ambulance screeched to a stop in front of her place, Madison stepped onto the porch. "In here." Madison motioned the EMTs inside. "He's downstairs to the left."

"We don't need to come in." The medical examiner's assistant waited on the porch. "Just direct us to the body, and we're fine."

"I'm afraid it's not that simple." Madison glanced over her shoulder. "Give me a second to make some hot tea for the man who fell through the ice, and I'll take you to the body. You're going to need generator lamps. And probably a sled and a pickaxe."

"We'll get our equipment."

Madison finished the tea and took it to Nate. "I'm showing the assistant ME where the body is."

"I can do that."

"No. You stay here. I'm good." She garbed up again and met the men on the porch. At least she thought they were all men. Until one of them gave her a quick hug.

"Good to see you again. Although I'd hope for better circumstances."

"Bernie." Madison reached for Detective Bernadette Santos. "We've got to stop meeting like this."

"First, shots fired at Oscar, and now a guy through the ice and a body under the ice." She shook her head as she walked beside Madison toward the lake. "Seems like you're at it again, my friend."

"Not me this time." Madison inclined her head toward the rental. "My neighbor, Alan Green, and his sister, Claire."

"Yeah. I heard her brother's missing."

"We may have found him." Madison stopped at the edge of the lake and faced the group of professionals behind her. "You'll need to set up your lights here on shore. The ice is thin in this area of the lake so I would suggest only one of you come out to the hole with me. You can decide how to recover the body after seeing what you're up against."

The assistant ME stepped forward. "I'll go with you."

She secured two more ropes to the pier and handed one to the young man beside her. "Tie it around your waist. We'll have to scoot out on our stomachs." She lowered herself onto the ice and waited for him to do likewise.

When they reached the hole, a thin layer of ice had already formed over the water. Her pick handle lay across the hole with the ski rope looped over it. She broke through the ice with a small hammer she'd brought and pulled on the rope.

"Let me." The assistant ME took hold of the rope and pulled. "There's something heavy attached to one end. A weight of some kind. I'm going to try to get the body to the surface."

Madison stared at the hole and prepared herself for the hideous sight to come.

But after a few minutes, the ME pulled the frayed end of the rope from the water. The body was gone.

14

Madison untied the rope at her waist and rubbed her arms. This reminded her too much of what happened all those years ago. A dead body by the lake at night. Only then there had been a watcher as well. Was there one now?

"I'll send some divers out in the morning." The assistant ME undid the rope around his waist and coiled it into a neat pile by the pier. "I don't imagine the body drifted too far."

"What happened?" Bernie asked.

"The body got loose and is somewhere under the ice." Madison started for the house. She needed to get inside, away from any unseen eyes in the darkness.

"I have a few more things to look at here. I'll join you in a moment." The young ME motioned to his crew to set up the arc lamps.

Bernie caught up to Madison. "It's not the same as last time."

"I know." She swept her eyes around the yard. "But I can't help it. Someone could be out there in the dark—watching."

"I understand." Bernie held the door for her.

The EMTs rolled the gurney out of the spare bedroom and

73

hefted it up the stairs. The man's eyes were closed, but his lips had regained their color.

"How is he?" Madison slid her arm through Nate's.

"He's going to be okay. He came to for a moment." Nate squeezed her arm. "He kept saying to tell Alan to be careful. His exact words were, 'Tell Alan, all in danger.'"

"Did you get his name?"

"His driver's license said Benjamin Delaney."

"There was a notation in Alan's journal about a meeting with *B* two days before Claire arrived."

"He's a little late for his appointment."

"True." Madison released his arm and climbed the stairs. "I guess we'll have to ask him when he feels up to it. Are you putting a guard outside his door?"

"Of course. He's a suspect in a kidnapping or possible murder, as far as I'm concerned."

"Nate, he didn't do it." She scoffed at him. "But he probably knows who did."

"Excuse me, but who's the detective in this family?"

"Why would he tell you to warn Alan if he knew he was already dead?"

"Madison, let me do my job. Remember our agreement?"

"You're right." She held up her hands in submission. "You're the police captain, and you have procedures to follow."

"Those procedures are there for a reason." He slid his arms around her waist. "To protect you and all the other good citizens of Pleasant Valley."

"I get it." She gave him a kiss. "And you do such a good job of it too."

Oscar woofed the familiar greeting he reserved for friends.

"I think I'll put him in the bedroom for now." Nate took the big dog by the collar and led him down the hall.

"Good idea." Madison opened the door to find Rafe, Jeannie, and Claire.

"I heard the calls on the radio. What's going on?" Jeannie

shrugged out of her coat and hung it on the coat tree. "Was that the guy who fell through the ice?"

"Yes." Madison helped Claire with her coat. "Good to see you again. Come in and let me make you a cup of tea."

"I saw divers out back." She turned anxious eyes on Madison.

Rafe caught Madison's arm. "I came back from helping load the poor guy on the ambulance to find these two on your porch." He held her until the others were out of earshot. "Is the dead guy Alan?"

"We're not sure." As she heated the water for tea, Madison closed her eyes. *Please give us the right words to say. Most of all, make us quick to listen and slow to speak.*

"Thank you." Claire wrapped her hands around the mug. "Jeannie told me you chased another intruder, and he fell through the ice. Then you had to save him. Was it the same guy you saw before?"

"No." Madison passed out cups of coffee to Rafe, Jeannie, and Nate. "I'd never seen this man before."

"Do you have any idea what's going on?" She took a tentative sip of the steaming brew.

"There's something in the house—or they think there's something in the house—they want," Nate said. "Do you have any idea what it might be?"

"No, none at all." Claire drained her cup.

"Let me make you another." Madison stood and went to the counter, thankful for the delay. She wasn't looking forward to telling her friend about the body they found.

"There's something else, Claire." Nate's tone was soft.

Tears formed behind Madison's eyes, and she grabbed a tissue to wipe them away before handing Claire another cup of tea.

"What is it?" She shifted her gaze from Madison to Nate, and it was clear she sensed bad news.

"As we were rescuing the man, we discovered a body under the ice."

Claire pushed her chair back as if putting distance between herself and his words would negate them. "You think it's Alan."

"They're not sure, but it could be." Rafe put an arm around her shoulders, but she shrugged it off.

"You knew?"

"No, but I found footage from the cameras at the house that shows him leaving through the back door with a man."

"Why didn't you tell me?" She gave him a hurt-filled look.

"I just got back from taking a copy to Jeannie."

"Does he look like he's going of his own accord, or is he ...?"

"He doesn't have a coat on, and the guy has a grip on Alan's arm."

She looked at Rafe with such raw pain Madison felt as if her own heart had been stabbed.

"Unfortunately, when I took the medical examiner out to determine how he was going to retrieve the body, it was gone. The rope failed, and the body sank beneath the ice again."

"He's still in the lake?" Claire's gaze shifted to the black night outside the kitchen windows.

"I'm afraid so."

"What are they doing about it?" Rafe asked.

"The police divers are coming tomorrow, but searching for a body under the ice is dangerous. There's no guarantee they'll be able to find him."

"I'll get cadaver dogs to help." Rafe straightened. "Let me know when to have them here."

"We'll take care of that." Jeannie shifted her angry gaze to Nate. "How did you let that happen?"

"We didn't *let* it happen." Madison fought to control the resentment in her tone. "Nate secured the rope. We were inside taking care of Benjamin, the man who fell through the ice. It was ten, fifteen minutes until help arrived."

"The rope must have been at the breaking point, and in the time we were away, it gave." Nate shook his head. "I tried."

"Sorry." Jeannie passed a hand over her face. "It's been a long day for all of us."

Claire was bent forward over the table with her forehead resting on her folded arms. Madison squatted next to her. "Why don't you go lie down on our daughter's bed for a while? I'll make some soup later." She helped the woman to her feet and guided her down the hall to a bedroom with off-white furniture and pale green walls.

Claire sat on the edge of the bed, and Madison took off her shoes. After Claire swung her legs onto the bed and arranged the pillows under her head, Madison tucked a patchwork quilt around the grieving woman. "Rest, my friend."

Madison slipped out of the room and into the hall before she let the tears pool in her eyes and trickle down her face. Urgent voices put her on alert. She wiped her face with her palms and returned to the kitchen.

"We found a cellphone." The assistant medical examiner held up an evidence bag. "It was in the shallow water at the edge of the lake next to the pier."

"Good work." Nate looked in the bag. "Anything else?"

"Only this." He held up a sodden bank book. "I'm not sure how much use it will be. We'll get them both to the lab right away."

"Whose is it?"

"I can't read the name."

"Tell them I said to put a rush on it." Nate followed the men to the front door.

Madison placed a pot on the stove and collected the ingredients for beef vegetable soup.

"Let me help." Rafe began peeling carrots. "Thanks for doing what you do."

"Which is?"

"Nurturing. Claire needs that."

"We all could use a little compassion once in a while." She dumped potatoes into the pot. "She needs you too."

"I'm not so sure."

"You can help her find out who killed her brother."

"*Took* my brother."

Madison spun around. Claire stood in the doorway with the quilt wrapped around her shoulders.

"Until we find his body, all we know is he was kidnapped." She took a seat at the table. "The soup smells wonderful. When do we eat?"

15

Claire gazed around the kitchen table at her new circle of friends. Now that they had proof Alan had been abducted, her focus became clear. Find him and bring him home. That was something she could do, something she'd been trained for. "Let's start with what needs to be done."

"A lot." Jeannie snorted and eyed Nate over her glasses. "Since this is now a kidnapping and possible homicide—"

"I think that's a reasonable assumption," he said.

"I disagree." Claire held up her hand. "Until there's concrete evidence, I think we treat it like a kidnapping."

"In either scenario, the first thing is to declare Alan's house a crime scene and get the forensics people over there." Jeannie gave Madison an expectant look. "Are you going to write this down?"

Madison did. "Claire can stay with us while that's being carried out." She looked up. "If she wants to?"

She nodded. The location was good, and she'd be in a position to hear the latest news on the case. "I know you"— Claire inclined her head toward Madison—"have notes on Alan's appointment journal, and so do I. We should pool those and organize the information."

Madison nodded as she wrote.

"If the cellphone and bank book are his, we'll get information from the lab that could help." Nate checked his phone. "Nothing yet, but I didn't expect it. When the divers retrieve the body tomorrow, we'll learn more."

"I hope so." Madison bit her lip. "Lake Pleasant can be difficult. It's fed by so many natural springs, and they produce underwater currents. They keep the lake healthy and cool in the summer, but those same currents might move a body away from where it was originally placed. Depending on its buoyancy."

"That's true, but I don't think the currents are very strong this time of year." Nate replaced his phone in his pocket.

"What else?" Claire scanned their faces. She didn't like thinking about the body moving under the ice. Or, if it was Alan, he may not be found until the spring thaw.

"I should hear more about Alan's other two buddies on the police force and Tommy Smith." Jeannie stretched and yawned. "We can add that to the mix."

"I still have the rest of the security tapes to review," Rafe said.

"And when we can interview Benjamin Delaney, we may get some answers we need." Nate stood, signaling the end of the meeting. "Time for bed. Or at least for a break. Go home. Everybody but Claire. Get some rest, and we'll see you in the morning."

Nate's face turned to stone. "Whoever is after what Alan has means business. Three different men have tried to enter the rental at night." His visage relaxed as he looked at Claire. "I'm glad you're staying here until we've had a chance to go through it."

Claire gathered the quilt to her chest. She wasn't used to all this kindness, which was hard for her to accept. Hard for her to show her appreciation. "Thank you."

MADISON TOOK her first cup of coffee for the day to the kitchen window. A layer of gray clouds held the promise of more snow later. She didn't envy the men who would be working in the frigid water this morning.

Oscar tapped his way across the wood floor to her side.

"Hi, big guy." She stroked his soft head and returned to the table where her Bible lay open to Psalms. She read from chapter 143, verse 8. "Let the morning bring me word of Your unfailing love for I have put my faith in You. Show me the way I should go for to You I lift up my soul."

Her gaze wandered to the list she'd made last night. Something about it seemed wrong. But what? She went over the conversation from the previous evening in her head. Everything people suggested was on the list.

She finished her devotional reading and prayers and made a fresh pot of coffee. Today would be busy.

Nate came up behind her and wrapped her in a warm hug. "You're up early."

"I couldn't sleep." She turned in his arms and kissed him. "Are you going to stick around for the divers?"

"Yes. I'll go into the office later." He looked out the window. "Not a great day for diving."

"Nate, I feel like we forgot to put something on the list." She opened the fridge door.

"I doubt it. We're a pretty thorough bunch."

"Still ..." She moved to the counter, broke eggs into a bowl, added a little milk, and whipped them into a creamy mix.

Claire walked into the kitchen. "Can I help?"

"You can set the table. I think there will be five for breakfast."

Oscar woofed and bounded from the kitchen, his tail on overdrive.

Madison turned from the stove with a bowl of scrambled eggs and almost caught Rafe in the head.

"Hey. You're taking my job." He pulled the silverware from Claire's hands and placed it next to the plates.

"You weren't here, and we were about to eat."

"Without me?" He placed a hand on his chest in mock horror.

Claire rolled her eyes at him and pulled out a chair.

Jeannie arrived a few minutes later. "The boys are right behind me. They're ready to play find the body."

The room got quiet, and Madison looked at Claire.

"I'm sorry. I didn't mean ..." Jeannie took a step toward Claire.

"It's okay." Claire rubbed her eyes. "I only hope they find it without too much trouble."

"We all do." Madison placed a hand on Claire's shoulder. Her heart ached for her new friend.

After everyone was seated, Nate said the blessing, adding a request that the Lord guide the men to the spot where the body lay and smooth the way for the recovery.

"Again, I'm really sorry, Claire," Jeannie said. "Sometimes I speak before I think."

"It's fine. Really. The body may not be Alan's." Claire gave her a smile. "Even if it is, if I want to be a part of finding out who killed him, I have to dissociate from him being my brother."

"That will be impossible." Nate shook his head. "You can be part of the case but within limits."

"Who sets the limits?" She set her fork down and glared at him.

"I do." He stared back.

Claire flung her napkin down and shoved her chair back.

"We have more to talk about." Nate stood.

"Give me a minute." She strode away.

Now it was Madison's turn to glare at her husband.

16

Madison rose. "Nate, sometimes I ..." She clamped her lips shut. "Drink your coffee. You need it." She hurried after Claire and knocked on the bedroom door. "Claire, may I come in?"

"Yes."

The grieving woman stood by the window, wrapped in the patchwork quilt.

Madison opened her mouth to speak but stopped, realizing this was one of those times when it was better to be present and silent.

"Nate's right." Claire brushed tears from her cheeks with her quilt-covered hands. "I'm too close to this case to expect to be a part of it."

"Maybe, but he could have been much more compassionate about how he told you." Madison put an arm around the woman.

Claire rested her head on Madison's shoulder and cried.

Madison gathered her in for a hug. "There, there. It will be all right." This woman was probably close to her age, but at that moment, her heart went out to Claire as if she were one of her children. "Hush now. Everything's going to be all right."

After several moments, Claire eased away from Madison. "Thank you. I haven't cried like that in so long."

"You've had a lot to deal with and needed to let it out."

"I did." Claire touched Madison's forearm. "You have something special. Something that makes me feel ... at peace."

Madison gave her a soft smile and touched her cross. "I think what you're seeing is my faith."

Claire reached a finger toward the silver cross. "I stopped believing long ago."

"Maybe it's time you start again."

"Maybe." She swiped once more at her eyes. "But first, I need to know what happened to Alan." She threw the quilt on the bed. "And I need to apologize to your husband."

"Oh, no." Madison wagged a finger. "He needs to apologize to you. Come on."

Back in the kitchen, Madison stood next to Claire.

"I'm sorry." Claire straightened. "You're right. I want to help in any way I can."

Madison pinned Nate with a glower.

"And I'm sorry for being so abrupt." Nate rose and came around the table. "I get into police mode and forget my compassion. Please forgive me." He held out his hand.

Claire gave it a shake.

Rafe stepped over to the kitchen window. "The divers are here."

Everyone gathered around him. Madison folded her arms around her waist as she watched the men in baggy red suits enter the icy water. Nate moved close and put his arm around her. She leaned into his warmth as a wave of sadness passed through her. Somewhere deep inside, she knew this was Alan. A dull pain throbbed in her chest.

After five long minutes, heads covered in black neoprene appeared again in the hole. They levered themselves out onto the ice and removed their air tanks. Without the body.

"We may as well get back to work. It may take them a couple

of dives to find him." Nate ushered the group back to the table. "Jeannie, check with the hospital on the status of Benjamin Delaney. Rafe, will you finish reviewing the security camera footage from the rental for the last two months? I'm going to find out what's keeping the forensics team."

Madison touched Claire's arm. "I'll make you a fresh cup of tea. Let's sit in the family room while they do their business. It's a lot more comfortable."

When the tea was finished, Madison carried two mugs into the other room, handed one to Claire, and settled into a matching recliner.

"You have such a nice house." Claire gazed around the room. "It's so warm and welcoming."

"Thanks. I want people to feel at home here."

"Where are your kids?"

"They went on a trip with their grandparents, Nate's mom and dad." Madison let her gaze settle across the room on a photograph of the twins. "I miss them."

"I bet you do. They're great-looking kids."

"They are. Do you want children someday?"

"Yes. When I meet the right man."

"No one special in your life now?" Madison knew she shouldn't pry, but she couldn't help herself.

Claire hesitated. "Not really. Rafe and I were close several years ago, but that relationship didn't end well."

"He still cares a great deal for you."

"I know." She averted her eyes. "I'm just not sure I can go through that pain again if it doesn't work out."

"That's a decision only you can make, but you could be passing up a chance at true happiness. How will you know if you don't try?"

"I just wish I knew for sure. How did you know Nate was the one?"

"I prayed a lot, and I mean a lot."

"I told you I stopped praying."

"Could be it's time to start again. Do you want me to help you?"

"I don't know." Claire furrowed her brow. "I guess it can't hurt."

"No, it won't." Madison chuckled. "Give me your hands." She bowed her head. "Lord, it's been a while since Your daughter has come to You in prayer, but I know You will hear the needs Claire puts before You. First of all, please help her find her brother, Alan. Second, please help her to understand Your will for her where Rafe is concerned. Should she pursue a relationship with him or not? Give her a sign. In Jesus' name, we pray. Amen."

Claire raised her face. Tears filled her eyes.

"That wasn't so bad, was it?"

Claire shook her head and smiled.

A shout went up from the other room. "The divers are coming up again. Looks like they've found him."

"Let's go." Madison squeezed Claire's hands.

17

Claire shot a look at Madison. Had the prayer worked? She bolted from the chair and into the kitchen in time to witness the red-suited divers slide the body onto the waiting sled. She needed to see if it was Alan.

As she turned from the window, she ran into a wall of flesh and muscle. Rafe blocked her way.

"I need to go." She pushed on his broad chest.

"No." He didn't budge. "Trust me."

"Rafe's right," Madison said. "I saw the body in the water, and if it's him, you don't want to remember him this way. Let Rose clean him up."

"Who's Rose?" Impatience mixed with frustration threatened to turn into rage inside her.

"The medical examiner."

She collapsed into a kitchen chair and put her head in her hands. Somehow, she knew the body they'd pulled from the lake was Alan. If only he'd gone to the authorities as soon as he discovered what was going on. She slammed the table with her fist. "You idiot. Now you're dead, and I'm alone."

Claire lifted her head, scanned the concerned faces of the

87

others, and groaned. "Sorry. I didn't mean to vent out loud. Alan was all the family I had left, and now he's gone."

"We may not be blood family, but we're here for you." Rafe slid onto the chair next to her. "*If* it's Alan, we'll find out who did this to him."

Nate's phone buzzed. "The forensics crew is next door. I'll be back."

"My notes are on the table. Would you get them for me?" Claire needed something to keep her mind off Alan. "Madison and I can compare what we discovered."

Nate frowned. "I will if the team hasn't logged them as evidence."

As she gazed out the window again, snowflakes tumbled out of the low gray clouds, obscuring her view of the lake. All this time, her brother's body could have been concealed within yards of where she ate and slept, and she hadn't sensed him. She bent over as if a blast of cold air had hit her from behind.

Madison set a plate of sandwiches and a bowl of apples on the table. "I know it's early, but it's been a stressful morning. I thought someone might need a little something to eat."

Claire's stomach gurgled. Maybe some protein would be good. She reached for a sandwich. Someone handed her a paper plate, a napkin, and a glass of iced tea. For right now, she should take life one bite at a time. With a little help from her friends.

After a time, Jeannie's phone buzzed. "Nate needs you and me"—she nodded at Claire—"over at the rental."

"Did they find something?" Claire jumped to her feet.

"He didn't say. Just come."

Claire took a couple of deep breaths before putting on her cold-weather gear. It could be something small. Or it could be major. No sense getting upset until she found out why he wanted her over there. But it was easier to tell herself that than to actually do it.

Nate met them at the front door of the rental. "Step inside

and put these suits on." He held out two white coveralls with booties. "Here are some gloves."

"My prints and hair will already be all over the house." Claire took one of the suits, stepped into the legs, and yanked the suit over her hips.

"Yes, but we don't want recent samples if we can help it." Nate led them to the garage. "The main thing I want to ask you about is the freezer."

She stared at the white rectangular box and flashed back to raising the freezer door the day she arrived. No Alan. He may have experienced a different kind of icy death, but he wasn't in the freezer.

"Claire." Jeannie nudged her arm. "Did you touch anything inside the freezer?"

"What? No." She shook her head. "I rested my arm on the edge there but didn't touch anything inside. It looked like someone gave him some venison or something."

"It's not meat." Nate grabbed a package and closed the lid. He unwrapped the white butcher paper and exposed a cellophane-wrapped bundle. As he unwrapped the plastic, it became clear what was inside. A stack of bills.

Jeannie whistled. "How much?"

"They're all hundreds." Nate set the stack on the freezer and fanned the edge of the bills. "We estimate around one hundred thousand dollars."

Claire stared at the pile of cash. "Alan, what have you done?"

"I'll have an officer get your things from upstairs." Nate directed them back inside.

"I can't stay here?"

"Not until forensics releases the house. That could be another couple of days."

She wasn't used to sharing space with another human being, much less two, but she understood. At least she would be able to keep tabs on the investigation. "Have they found his computer yet?"

"I don't think so. I'll check." Nate nodded at Jeannie.

"Can I at least take my brother's appointment book and my notes?"

"I'll get them." Nate retrieved the worn journal and her papers. "I'll see you later."

"One more thing. My car. Since whatever happened to Alan seems to have taken place before I got here, I should be able to have my car."

"It's better off in the garage than outside."

"Fine. As long as I can get to it whenever I want to."

Nate ran a hand through his hair. "That could be a problem. Let me see what else I can come up with."

"Let's go." Jeannie zipped her coat and pulled a watch cap over her head. "It's snowing again." Her voice was almost a growl. "I hate snow."

If this were a normal visit with her brother, Claire would have loved the snow and the feeling of being cut off from the world with all its problems. She and Alan would have sat by the fire and reminisced about their childhood, ate all the food he'd packed into his refrigerator, and read books. She never had time to read.

Instead, she found herself in his neighbor's house, eating his neighbor's food, and the only reading she was doing had to do with Alan's kidnapping and possible murder. "I hate snow too."

And she knew that hatred would last for the rest of her life.

Back at Madison's house, Claire begged off sharing a tea with her new friend saying she had a headache and needed to lie down. Which was true to some degree. What she really needed was time and space to think.

If she allowed the investigation to run its course, who knew what they would discover about Alan that could damage his reputation. She needed to find out for herself before the police did. If for no reason other than to ensure he got dealt with fairly. How could she accomplish that without jeopardizing her job or hurting anyone else?

She stretched out on the bed and flipped through Alan's journal. A word paired with a notation caught her eye. She'd found the location of Alan's lockbox. Here was something she could do, but two other things needed to happen for her plan to succeed. The first was already set in motion, but the second would be tricky.

18

Claire stayed in her room until supper. The sight of three place settings at the table filled her with relief tinged with disappointment. "Rafe isn't joining us tonight?"

"There you are." Madison pulled a roasted chicken from the oven.

The savory smells made Claire's stomach growl.

"He's taking night security duty so one of his men can spend time with his family, and Jeannie's got a date night with her husband."

Family, date nights, and cooking for a husband. Would her life ever be like that? Claire expelled a sigh. "Can I help with anything?"

"You can get the drinks. I'll have tea, and Nate likes water."

Nate walked into the kitchen as she finished placing the glasses. "I brought you one of Alan's garage door openers. The code has been disabled. You're free to use your car whenever you want." He pulled the opener from his coat pocket and set it on the counter.

"Thanks." One obstacle cleared. "I appreciate it."

"You're welcome." He collapsed onto a chair and gulped

down half a glass of water. "Dinner sure smells good. When do we eat?"

"It won't be long." Madison turned from the stove. "But do you think it's a good idea for Claire to be out on her own?"

"No, but we're not her parents." Nate passed a hand down his face. "And I'm pretty sure the bad guys aren't after her. They want what we found in the house this afternoon."

"What did you find?"

"Ninety-eight thousand dollars in one-hundred-dollar bills wrapped in butcher paper and stockpiled in the freezer." He took another drink. "Which we now have securely stored at the police station."

"Wow." Madison shook her head. "That's a lot of cash. Where in the world did Alan get that much money?"

"We'll talk about it later."

"It's okay." Claire stared into her glass of tea. "We all know there's no way Alan saved that much money from his police pension, no matter how frugal he was."

"Maybe he had some investments?" Madison sat a platter of chicken on the table. "Or maybe he was working with some other agency like Rafe suggested."

"I would have known about it." She took a drink. "I've tried to rationalize all the things we've discovered, but the fact is Alan got himself mixed up in something, and it got him killed. I think he begged me to come because he wanted help getting out from whatever he was involved in, but I was too late."

"That may be the case," Nate said in a quiet voice. "But the money came up clean. No drug residue, and the serial numbers are okay." He rubbed the back of his neck. "So, as far as the police are concerned, it's Alan's free and clear. Unless we find out otherwise. We'll keep it safe until you decide what you want to do with it. If you're okay with that."

"Yes, thank you." Claire's stomach clenched at the thought of making a decision about so much money. "If you don't mind, I'd like to eat, and then I think I'll go to bed." She mustered a small smile.

"Of course, sweetheart." Madison set the rest of the food on the table and pulled out a chair.

After dinner, Claire excused herself to her bedroom and placed the garage door next to the clothes she'd laid out for tomorrow. In the morning, she would set her plan in motion. Now, she would sleep.

EARLY MORNING LIGHT filtered through the curtains. Claire dressed quickly. After checking to see that Madison and Nate's door was closed, she eased down the hall. Oscar met her in the living room, his tail wagging a greeting.

"It's okay." She motioned him back to the kitchen. "Go back to your rug." When he obeyed, she slipped out into the new day.

Weak winter sunlight reflected off low gray clouds. The snow had stopped, but the frigid air sucked moisture from every inch of her exposed flesh. She hurried across the lawns to Alan's garage.

She cringed as the creaking and popping of the garage door echoed across the frozen landscape. The SUV started on the first try. She backed out of the garage and pressed the button. This time, she didn't stick around for the noise. At the top of the hill, she turned left toward the police station and her next objective.

Jeannie's car was in the parking lot. Did the woman ever sleep? Claire entered the station and placed her credentials on the counter. "I need to talk to Detective Jansen."

"Who are you?" The officer manning the front desk glanced at her ID.

"Homeland Security Analyst Claire Green."

He didn't blink an eye. "What's this about?"

She pressed her lips together. Patience. "She'll know. We spoke earlier."

"I need to write something on the ledger."

"The Mathis Thoms murder case." Maybe that would get a reaction. Nothing.

"I'll let her know you're here. Take a seat."

Take a seat? Claire plopped into the chair closest to the information desk. Within moments, the door swung open, and Jeannie greeted her with a hug.

"Sorry about the gatekeeper. If I'd known you were coming, I would have met you in the foyer." Jeannie led her through into the squad room and motioned her into the chair she sat in before. "What's up? No Rafe?"

"No." She folded her hands in her lap. "This is something I want to do on my own."

"Okay." Jeannie gave her a puzzled look.

"I need Alan's safe deposit box key back."

The detective scratched her nose. "Claire, I'm not sure—"

"Have you identified the body from the lake as my brother?"

"No, not yet. Rose will be working on him today."

"Is my brother an official suspect in the Thoms murder?"

"No, but—"

"Since I haven't filed an official missing persons report with the police, the key is still technically my possession, and I want it back."

"What's going on?" Jeannie tapped a finger on her desk. "Does Rafe know you're here?"

"No. He's—" There was an edge of frustration in her voice, and she willed it away. "No, he doesn't."

Jeannie studied her a moment longer before opening her drawer, withdrawing the key, and sliding it across the desk to her. "So, where is Alan's box?"

Claire stood and slipped the key into her pocket. "Thanks, Detective Jansen. I appreciate the time and effort you've put in on my brother's disappearance."

"Not going to answer my question?" Jeannie rose. "I'll just say this. You're making a mistake. Especially where Rafe is concerned."

"Maybe. But ... maybe." The second hurdle cleared. Now for the most difficult part.

RAFE TOWELED the sweat from his face and answered his phone. "What's up?"

"Claire's left." Madison's frantic voice resounded over the speaker.

"What do you mean left?"

"I got up to make coffee and saw her driving out of the neighborhood."

"When was this?" He yanked a T-shirt over his head and pulled on his jeans from last night.

"About ten minutes ago."

"I'm coming over." He pressed End. What was Claire up to? He yanked on his boots, pushed his arms into his parka, and slammed out of the house.

Madison met him at the door. "She's wearing her gray suit."

"Which means?"

"She's being professional today. Or wants someone to think she's acting in a professional capacity."

"Good catch." Rafe hurried to Claire's bedroom. "Anything else?"

"Alan's journal." Madison picked it up. "It was open to this page, and look what Claire wrote."

"Ross County Banking Center, Chillicothe." Rafe's phone rang, and he glanced at the screen. "Jeannie. What is it?"

"I had a visitor this morning."

"Let me guess. Claire." His hand tightened around his cell phone. "Did you give her the key?"

"I had no choice, but how did you know?"

"I'll tell you later. When did she leave?"

"About ten minutes ago."

He checked his watch. "She's headed for Chillicothe. I need to get there before she does. Can you let patrol know I'll be on the road?"

"I'll do better. I'll drive you. Meet me at the gas station." She hung up.

Jeannie didn't have to tell him which one. "Got to go, Madison."

"Keep me informed."

He nodded and sprinted to his car.

The streets were plowed for the most part, and he made good time. As soon as he clicked his buckle in the police SUV, Jeannie took off.

"What's the plan?" She merged into traffic and floored the accelerator.

"Catch her before she enters the bank." Rafe suppressed a shudder as Jeannie slipped between two semis into the fast lane.

"If we weren't in a hurry, I'd give that guy a speeding ticket." She glared in her rearview mirror and shot forward. "What if we're not in time?"

"I haven't gotten that far." He forced himself to relax.

19

Claire plugged the address into her phone's GPS. She wasn't used to driving on snowy roads, so she slowed to a crawl once she left the Pleasant Valley city limits. She relaxed when she spotted the sign welcoming her to Chillicothe, Ohio.

All she had to do now was find the bank and convince them to let her into Alan's safe deposit box. She groaned. Should she tell the truth and play on their emotions, or lie and hope she didn't get caught? Neither game plan held out much chance for success.

The Chillicothe branch of Ross County Banking Center sat on a corner. She liked the look of it—friendly somehow. Her spirits buoyed, Claire entered through the double doors and strode across to the desk marked Safe-Deposit Box Sign In.

She held out her credentials. "I'm Homeland Security Agent Claire Green. I need to speak to your manager."

The young woman consulted her computer, and her face brightened with a smile. "Of course, Miss Green. Right this way."

She drew on all of her training to keep the look of surprise from her face. It was as if they had been expecting her. But why?

Had Jeannie known where she was going all along and called ahead? She followed the woman to an office down a short hall.

"Miss Green is here." The woman smiled at her again and left.

A pudgy man in a navy blazer stood and extended his hand. "Nice to finally meet you, Miss Green. Or do you prefer Agent Green?"

"Either is fine." She sat and crossed her legs.

"Your brother talks about you often." The man consulted some notes on his desk.

She uncrossed her legs and clenched her hands in her lap to keep from badgering him with questions. What had Alan said about her? When did the manager last speak to him?

"He insisted you be allowed access to his security box." The man smiled. "He explained you travel a great deal and would have trouble getting here to sign the paperwork, but asked us to accommodate you when you showed up."

What did he say? "I'm sorry. I didn't catch that. I'm ... tired."

"He said we were to let you into his safe deposit box. It's irregular, but your brother has been a loyal customer of ours for many years, and we are more of a family here." He waved his arm around in a circle. "Small town. You know."

She nodded. She was beginning to understand small towns and liked what she saw.

"All we need from you is your signature and a copy of your ID for the file." He held out his hand for her credentials.

"Of course." She gave him her driver's license and her Homeland Security identification.

He rose and left the room. Claire sat very still. No doubt cameras were recording her every move, and she must appear calm. This was all routine. Nothing out of the ordinary.

No note behind a picture that hinted at serious trouble. No money in a freezer. And no frozen body that could possibly be her brother. She relaxed her hands.

"Here we are." The bank manager handed her a key. "Shall we?"

As he led her to the vault, she slid her left hand into her pocket and fingered the jagged edges of Alan's key. If only she'd known. The whole scene with Jeannie was unnecessary. The manager inserted his key into the door numbered two hundred twenty-five and moved aside for Claire to fit her key into the second lock.

He withdrew the box, pulled out a shelf, and set the key there before stepping to the side. "Would you like to take it to a booth, or are you okay with doing your business here?"

"I'm fine here."

A woman stuck her head inside the vault. "One of the tellers needs you."

He nodded and turned to Claire. "I'll only be a moment."

She waited for him to leave and scanned the vault. Cameras were mounted in two corners. She should have gone to a booth.

Too late now. She positioned her body to block one camera and opened the box, hoping the lid would block the other. An envelope addressed to her lay on top. She lifted it out and felt something hard inside. She folded the envelope around the object and stuck the small package in her purse.

Before closing the box, she sifted through the remaining contents. The lease to the rental house, the title to her brother's SUV, and his retirement papers were stacked in an orderly fashion. His birth certificate was on the bottom of the pile. She swiped the tears from her eyes and jammed that document into her purse.

But what she found underneath the papers dried her tears and sent a stabbing pain through her chest. Five thousand dollars in one-hundred-dollar bills. "Oh, Alan," she whispered. "What have you gotten yourself mixed up in?" She covered the money with the other documents and secured the lid.

"All finished?" The manager entered the vault again. "Did you find what you needed?"

"Yes, thank you again." She handed him the box, and they went through the procedure of securing it again. "Is there a restroom I can use before making the drive back?"

"Certainly." He motioned her ahead of him. "Let me show you."

As she washed her hands, her phone dinged.

"CLAIRE DRIVES A GRAY SUV." Rafe scanned the bank parking lot. "Looks like we've beaten her here."

Jeannie had parked with a line of sight to both the front and side of the building.

"No, there she is." Jeannie pointed out the windshield.

Claire parked on the side of the bank close to the front and headed for the entrance.

Rafe released his seatbelt and reached for the door handle.

"Wait." Jeannie grabbed his arm.

"Wait? Why?" Rafe kept his eyes on Claire as she walked into the bank. "We should stop her before she tries to get into Alan's box."

Jeannie shook her head. "I got a feeling about this. Let's see what happens."

Rafe huffed and stared at the front door of the bank.

"If they refuse to let her into the box, she should be out in five, ten minutes." Jeannie looked at her watch. "If she's in there longer, then for some reason, they gave her access, and I'd like to know why."

He wasn't good at waiting, so he usually assigned one of his employees to stakeouts. But Jeannie had a point, and he was curious too.

Cars came and went. An SUV parked next to Claire, blocking their view of her vehicle, but left a few minutes later. A few minutes later, a panel van backed into the same space.

It was coming up on ten minutes. No Claire. "She's in."

"Yeah. I wonder if her brother's in there with her."

"You think he's still alive?" Rafe swiveled his focus to Jeannie.

"Makes the most sense." She shrugged. "He could be hiding a gun and accessing cash and a new identity to make a getaway."

"Claire would never go along with that." Rafe glared at Jeannie.

"He's her brother. You'll do a lot for family you wouldn't even consider for someone else."

"I don't care if he's ..." But Jeannie was right. He couldn't think of anyone Claire would be more inclined to help than her brother. Not him, for sure. Maybe Jeannie was right. But he prayed she was wrong. Rafe inclined his head toward the entrance. "Look, she's coming out."

Claire walked around the corner of the bank and passed the panel van on the way to her SUV.

The van backed out and left, but her car was still there. Empty. No sign of Claire.

"Something's wrong." He scrambled out of Jeannie's vehicle before she could stop him again. A sudden urgency had him jogging across the parking lot and bursting into the bank. He searched the space for any sign of Claire.

"Take it easy, man." Jeannie caught up with him. "They're going to think you're here to rob the place."

He blinked and noticed the startled faces around him. "Sorry. I'm looking for my friend."

"Let's try over there." Jeannie pointed to the desk with a Safe-Deposit Box sign.

"May I help you?" The young woman gave them a stiff smile. One of her hands remained out of sight.

Jeannie displayed her badge, and the young woman relaxed. "We're looking for Claire Green."

"I'm afraid you just missed her."

"Her car's still outside."

"All I know is I saw her walk out the door." The woman gestured at the glass entry door thirty feet across the lobby.

"Thanks." Rafe hurried through the door. No Claire. He strode toward her SUV. In the spot where the van stood, he glanced down. "Jeannie, look at this." A folded envelope with Claire's name on it stuck to the damp pavement. He bent to pick it up.

"Don't." Jeannie grabbed his arm. "It's evidence."

"She's gone." Rafe glared at Jeannie. "I wanted to go in after her, but you stopped me. Now they've got her." She flinched. His words had hit home. But he didn't care.

"I'm sorry. It was a bad call." Jeannie straightened. She handed Rafe an evidence bag. "Now, let's concentrate on getting her back." She turned and reentered the bank.

He had to get past his anger. It blocked him from moving forward, from doing what he did best. "I can't do this alone. I need Your help." Rafe lifted his face to the sky. His eyes landed on the camera at the corner of the building. "Thank you." He put the envelope into the evidence bag and joined Jeannie inside.

After a heated discussion between Jeannie and the manager, Rafe followed them to a back room. The three of them reviewed the last twenty minutes of the security footage. Claire hadn't gone willingly. Two men wearing ski masks and gloves jumped from the van's side door. One jammed a hand over her mouth while the other pressed a needle into her arm. She had the presence of mind to drag the envelope from her coat pocket and drop it before they dragged her into the van.

"I'm calling Nate." Jeannie whipped out her phone. "He can get a local team over here."

Rafe found it hard to swallow around the lump lodged in his throat. And when the police arrived and asked for his statement, he could barely sit still. Claire was out there somewhere having who knows what done to her, and here he was doing nothing.

"I think that's all we need for now." The officer closed his book. "Thanks for your cooperation."

He stood, shook the guy's hand, and bolted for the door. Jeannie waited for him in the car. "Did you get copies of the tapes from the vault and the outside camera?"

"Yep." She hit the gas pedal. "Let's go find your girl."

20

Claire swiped the spittle from her mouth and fought the van's rocking as she pushed to a seated position within the moving van. "What's this all about? Do you have my brother? I want to see him."

The man across from her glanced at the driver. "Soon."

"Kidnapping is bad enough, but kidnapping a federal agent is … well, that's a whole other ballgame." She gave a slow shake of her head. "You'll get the chair for this."

The man's confident look changed to one of uncertainty. He glanced at his partner again.

"Shut your mouth, or I'll have my buddy give you another shot," the driver said.

Claire shrugged and averted her gaze as if she'd said all she had to say. Inside, her stomach churned as she went through options for escape. And possible weapons at hand. Like the wrench to her right, probably overlooked because it was the same color as the floor.

She couldn't see much of the driver, but the man across from her looked like he was in his early twenties. Caucasian, with a trim beard and mustache. Slim, but strong. The only advantage she would have would be surprise and the fact that if she could get past the one in back and out the door, she was fast and could probably outrun the driver.

"The boss says to put the stick into the computer and make sure it's the right one." The driver glanced back over his shoulder at the man in back.

"Okay." The young man in back with her opened a laptop and inserted the flash drive. A frown furrowed his brow. "It's encrypted."

"Ask her what the password is."

The bearded young man looked at her. "You heard him."

"How should I know? It's my brother's flash drive. Have him tell you the code."

"We—" The man pressed his lips together. "It's not that simple."

Something crumbled in Claire's chest. "What do you mean it's not that simple?" She pinned him with her gaze.

"He can't talk right now." The driver's tone made it clear he was losing his patience.

"I have no idea what his password would be." But she did know the password to the memory stick plugged into the computer on the younger man's lap because she'd switched one of hers for Alan's in the restroom. She shifted her position. The reassuring pressure to her inner thigh let her know she still possessed her brother's flash drive. Which she doubted he'd encrypted.

"Guess." The harsh voice of the driver reverberated through the van.

She made a show of thinking. "Try his birthday. Eleven, seven, seventy."

"Nope."

"My brother's not a complicated guy. How about the day he retired from the force?" She gave him the numbers.

The young kidnapper shook his head.

Claire knew that after three tries, the memory stick he had in the computer would lock for twenty-four hours. She'd set it up that way. One more try. "My nickname? Greeniebeanie?"

"Wait," the driver said. "Don't try again until we get to the boss."

The bearded man shut the computer and put the flash drive in his pocket.

Claire bit her lip. So close. She inched her hand closer to the wrench and waited for a stop sign or a red light.

RAFE WASN'T happy when Jeannie insisted they return to the Pleasant Valley police station, but she had a point. They had no idea which direction the van had gone, and until they did, they might as well head back.

At the station, Rafe sat beside Jeannie at her desk as they reviewed the video of the men abducting Claire. It happened in a matter of seconds. She had no opportunity to fight back. He clenched his hands into rock-hard fists scarred from use.

As the van drove away, Jeannie paused the video. "It's blurry, but I think Bulldog can do something with it. I'll get it to him ASAP."

"Bulldog?" He eyed Jeannie and relaxed his fingers.

"You know. Randy over in Tech Support. He's a magician when it comes to computer stuff."

"Yeah. Tell him it's urgent."

"He'll know." She pressed Send.

"Have they processed the envelope yet?" Rafe rubbed his forehead. He wanted to be doing something. Anything. Sitting here drove him mad.

"Yes. There was a letter inside." Jeannie laid photocopies of both on the desk in front of him. "From Alan to Claire."

He scanned the letter.

Dear Claire,

If you're reading this, I'm probably dead. Please don't be sad. I had a good life, and I loved you. I only hope you'll still love me after you see what's on this drive. Let me say in my defense that I never spent a penny of the money, and when you read my will, you'll discover my instructions on how to distribute my frozen assets. I am leaving five thousand in cash for you. Don't worry. It's all mine. Although I guess you will want to pay taxes on it knowing how by the book you are. Just kidding. That's it for now. Everything you need is on the flash drive. Be careful, sis. I love you.

Alan

"What's this about frozen assets?" Rafe pointed to the line in the note.

"I have no idea. I didn't think Alan had much in the way of assets, period."

"Me either." Rafe picked up the evidence bag with the envelope in it. "How did she talk her way into the lockbox?"

"She didn't have to. The manager had written instructions from Alan. He wanted Claire to have access to his box, and they agreed to wait until she could get there to sign the papers and give them a copy of her identification."

"Is that usual banking procedure?"

"He kept saying they're more than a bank. They're a family."

"If Alan's alive, they could be holding him against his will. Like Claire."

"Possible." She tapped the letter. "The question then becomes what's on this flash drive that's so valuable someone would kill one man and kidnap one, maybe two, other people to get it?"

"You think the death of Mathis Thoms is linked to the kidnappings?" Rafe asked.

"I'm sure of it."

A stone-cold rage swept through him. Claire had come back into his life after five long years, and he was not about to lose her again.

THEY WERE out of the country and into traffic again. Claire's instinct warned her they neared their destination. If she didn't move fast, she may not get the opportunity to escape. The van stopped at a light, but it turned green, and they were off again. Too quick.

She cut her eyes between the driver and the bearded man across from her. Both men sat rigid and alert. They must be getting close. The van slowed again.

When it stopped for another light, she grabbed the wrench and swung it at the bearded man's head. A cry followed a terrible crunching sound. The driver swiveled in his seat. His fingers pinched the back of her shirt, but she pulled free and headed for the back doors. The van lurched forward, and she fell. A horn sounded. The driver cursed.

She crawled to the doors and flung them open just as the van heaved forward again. The hood of the car behind them broke her fall. She rolled off and sprinted in the opposite direction. At first, fear blotted out everything around her, but she forced herself to glance back. The light turned green, and the van turned right.

Think. What would she do if she were them? Turn around or drive around the block and try to cut her off? In either case, she needed to do the unexpected. She swerved to her right and crossed the busy street, dodging through cars and trucks to gain the opposite side. A coffee shop was tucked in between a bookstore and a boutique. She stepped inside and chose a seat with a view of the street.

Several minutes later, the van passed slowly in front of the restaurant. The bearded man sat in the passenger's seat, scanning the crowd. She scrunched down in her chair and lowered her head.

"You look lost."

"What?" Claire whipped her head around.

"I said, you look lost." A balding man sat at the table next to her and held a menu. "Do you need help?"

"No—I mean, yes, but there's nothing you can do for me."

"Try me."

"I'm Homeland Security Agent Claire Green, and I just escaped from two men in a white van. Unless you're law enforcement, you really shouldn't get involved."

The man's brown eyes grew wide. "I can call the police." He dug his phone out of his jacket pocket and dialed.

"Thank you." Claire joined him at his table. "Now you can buy me a cup of hot tea. Earl Grey. One sugar. And ask the manager to join us."

After apologizing to the manager for the police, firefighters, and EMTs about to descend on his shop, Claire sipped her tea and eyed the man across from her. He shifted in his chair. "I'd say you could leave, but I know the police will want to speak to you since you made the call. Sorry."

"That's okay." He threw her a brief smile. "Are all the days of a Homeland Security Agent so exciting?"

She chuckled. "No. Most are pretty boring."

"Do you think you might want to go out for a drink on one of your boring days?"

Rafe's face filled her mind. "I'm in a relationship. Sorry."

"I'm not surprised." He lifted his coffee cup to his lips.

The faint scream of sirens reached her ears.

"Maybe we should wait for the police outside?" the man asked. "It might be less disturbing for the other customers.

"Good idea." She nodded and stood.

He held the door for her and guided her away from the

restaurant's windows toward a bench. But a few steps along the sidewalk, he gripped her arm and thrust something solid against her side. "Keep walking. You wouldn't want to die right here on the sidewalk after all you've gone through to live, would you?"

21

Claire struggled against his grasp. "How did you find me?"

"I was following those numbskulls from the time they grabbed you at the bank." He yanked her arm behind her back at a painful angle. "It must have hurt when you landed on the hood of that car."

"Not so much." She willed herself to speak at a normal pitch as the pain stabbed her shoulder.

Around the corner, the white van idled at the curb. The bearded man and the driver jumped out and grabbed her.

"Tie her up this time, you idiots." The man from the restaurant took a step back and lowered his weapon.

Claire only had a split second to act. One thing was sure. She was not getting back in the van with those men. She sunk her teeth into the bearded man's hand. He uttered a curse and let go of her. She swiveled and delivered a kick to his chest that sent him sprawling. Without pause, she turned to the driver and drove her knee between his legs. He released her and doubled over in agony.

The bald man from the restaurant moved toward her, gun in hand. She jumped into the van, slammed the side door, and squirmed into the driver's seat. The passenger door opened. She wrenched the van into drive, yanked the wheel to the left, and stepped on the gas.

The van lurched forward and caught the back fender of the car parked in front of it. She glanced over as the passenger door banged shut on the man from the restaurant. He screamed and fell to the pavement. Claire laid on the horn and raced through the intersection, pressing the accelerator to the floor. She had no idea where she was or how to find the police.

One thing she knew for sure. If she kept driving like a mad woman, the police would come to her. She headed the wrong way down a one-way street. When she turned onto Main Street, she steered the large vehicle onto the wrong side of the road. It didn't take long. Soon, the sweet sound of sirens filled the air.

She pulled to the side. Two police cars skidded to a stop behind her, and four police officers emerged with guns drawn.

"Put your hands out the window," they repeatedly said in loud voices.

She complied with a smile on her face.

One officer yanked the driver's door open and pulled her out. "On the ground. You think it's funny, do you?"

"No, sir, I'm just glad to see you."

"Now I've heard everything. Do you have any weapons?"

"Not that I know of." Her arms shook with the release of adrenaline.

"Are you getting smart with me?"

"No, sir. I don't know what's in the van. I stole it from my kidnappers."

"Who the blazes are you?"

"Homeland Security Agent Claire Green." She gave a slight nod toward the van. "I think my purse is still in there."

The officer spoke into his shoulder communicator.

"Sarge. There's a purse in here with an ID." The officer came around to show the first officer. "It looks like her." He inclined his head toward Claire.

"Keep an eye on her." Sarge stepped away and had a brief

conversation with someone on his phone. When he returned, he held out his hand to help her. "Seems you're telling me the truth, Agent Green. But you still caused a lot of problems for us."

"I know, and I'm sorry about that, but I have no idea where I'm at or where the police station is. It was the only way I could think to get your attention."

"You're in Washington, Ohio." He eyed her. "You must be the young woman I got the report about earlier today who jumped out of a van and landed on poor Mrs. Landry's car at the stoplight."

"Yes. I managed to escape only to accept help from a man who was in league with my kidnappers." She pulled her jacket tighter around herself. "My rotten luck. Could we sit in your car? I'm freezing."

Sarge led the way to his police car. "You'll have to sit in the back."

"That's okay. As long as it's warm." Once inside, she wasn't so sure. The vehicle was warm, but the smell of stale beer, unwashed bodies, and other bodily fluids made her want to continue their conversation outside.

"I'll take you to the station house, where you can wait for your friends."

She jerked her head up. "Friends?"

"Detective Jansen and Rafe O'Connell?" He caught her eye in the rearview mirror. "Detective Jansen put out an all-points bulletin on the van and you. She was mighty glad to hear we found you. And Mr. O'Connell promised to take care of any damages you caused on your driving spree."

"He did?" She swallowed and blinked away the tears forming in her eyes. No way did she want a stranger—especially another professional—to witness her getting emotional.

At the station, Sarge led her to his desk. "I've put out a BOLO based on your descriptions of your kidnappers and the man at the café. With any luck, we'll have them soon."

"Thanks." But somehow, she wasn't convinced finding the

men would be that easy. Whoever was behind everything had a backup plan—the bald guy at the café. The people she was up against were smart. "You might find something on their computer."

"What computer?"

"The one in the van."

"The only thing we found in the van was your purse. Oh, and this." Sarge laid Rafe's gun on his desk.

22

Rafe stared at Jeannie as she spoke on the phone. When she rose and pulled her coat from the back of her chair, he knew. They'd found Claire or the van or both. He stood and zipped his jacket, ready to go.

She stuffed her cell phone in her pocket. "Claire's in Washington. Just north of here."

"Is she okay?" His voice was husky with emotion he couldn't suppress.

"Yeah. She's at the police station. I'll give you the details on the way."

Sunlight glinted off the snow, and a few white clouds dotted the blue sky. He hadn't noticed what a great day it was until now. Even Jeannie's account of how Claire fought off the men and stole the van didn't dampen his good mood. She was safe. That was all that mattered.

When they arrived at the Washington PD, the guy Jeannie called Sarge met them at the door. "We're back here." He glanced at her. "We've met before."

"At a state training class a few years ago in Cincinnati."

He snapped his fingers. "That's right. You were the feisty one."

Rafe coughed to cover a laugh, and Jeannie glared at him.

"Agent Green is over there." Sarge tipped his head forward and to the left.

Claire sat with her back to them, her face in profile. Her shoulders sagged, and her face looked gaunt. It was all Rafe could do not to rush over and pull her into his arms, but she'd hate it if he did. Not here. Maybe not ever again.

"Mr. O'Connell, I hope you can clear up something for me." Sarge led the way to his desk.

What could he want with him? He followed, and when he reached Claire, he touched her shoulder gently. "I'll be glad to help any way I can."

"Agent Green claims this is your gun, which was stolen from her brother's house a few nights ago." Sarge pointed to the pistol lying on his desk.

Rafe eyed the weapon. "It looks like mine. Can I see it?"

Sarge lifted the pistol with the cloth it was wrapped in and handed the weapon to Rafe. "Be careful. We need to preserve fingerprints, you know."

"I understand." Rafe did a quick examination of the gun. "It's mine."

"Which means it's the weapon used in a homicide in my district," Jeannie said.

"That's what Agent Green was telling me." Sarge wrapped the gun away again. "I'm sure you won't mind if we fingerprint it before passing it on to you?"

"No. As long as you make it quick."

"I'll send it to the lab now." He motioned an officer over and instructed him to take the gun straight to the lab.

"You said you had descriptions of the men who kidnapped Agent Green?" Jeannie pulled up a chair. "Would you text those to me? Please?"

"I've put out a state-wide BOLO. You should have access to that, but I'll gladly send you the descriptions if you like."

"I would." She opened her phone and flipped through her

photos to one of the men Madison caught on video. "Does this guy look familiar to you?" She handed it to Sarge.

He enlarged it with his fingers and studied it for a long moment. "No, can't say I've ever seen him around." He handed her phone back. "What's he done?"

"He's been snooping around Claire—Agent Green's rental."

"Sounds like you've made a few enemies, Agent." Sarge raised his brow at her.

"Not me, my brother. But they're mine now, and they'll be sorry."

Rafe didn't like the look in Claire's eyes. He placed a hand on her forearm. The rock-hard muscles relaxed with his touch. "You're not in this alone."

She blinked. "That's what I meant. Now they've got the police and many others on their trail."

But he didn't believe her, and it worried him.

FINALLY, a text from Rafe. "Claire was kidnapped?" Madison dumped the journal on the floor and jumped to her feet. She paced to the kitchen as she read. "Oh, thank God. She's okay." She didn't know whether to strangle him for not letting her know or be thankful he hadn't. She would have been a nervous wreck waiting for news.

Oscar tapped his way across the wooden floors in Madison's shadow. When she stopped in front of the refrigerator, he sat and cocked his head.

"I'm okay, boy." She ruffled his ears and removed the pitcher of iced tea. Her hand shook as she poured herself a big glass. A sudden sadness washed over her.

In the past, she would have been in the middle of all the action. Receiving the latest updates. Helping search for the kidnappers. But not anymore.

Was this how her life should be? Nate was certainly happier

now. He didn't have to worry about her as much. Had she made the excitement of her job a sort of idol? The place where she found her meaning? Heavy questions that would require heavier prayer.

Her phone chimed, and Nate's face filled her screen. "Hello, my wonderful husband."

"You may not think I'm so wonderful once you've heard my news."

"What is it?" Her mind raced through several terrible scenarios, most of which involved the kids and an accident.

"The body from the lake is Alan Green."

Relief flooded her brain immediately, followed by guilt. "Poor Claire."

"I think she suspected from the moment we discovered him, but that doesn't make it any easier."

"How did he die?"

"He was shot, weighed down with a cinder block, and thrown into the lake."

"Why didn't we hear the gunshot?" She walked to the kitchen window and stared at the place where the divers had pulled the body from the ice.

"The perp probably used a silencer. The bullet placements look professional."

"Have you told Claire yet?"

"No. She's ..." He paused.

"I know about the kidnapping." She couldn't control the quaver in her voice. "Rafe texted me."

"Claire's fine, sweetheart."

Madison closed her eyes and let her husband's comforting words sink into her soul.

"But she'll be busy with the Washington PD. There's time enough to tell her later—after Jeannie and Rafe bring her home," Nate said.

Madison slumped into a kitchen chair. "I love you, Nate Zuberi."

"Love you—" A man shouted Nate's name in the background. "Madison, Delaney woke up and wants to talk. I want you with me when I speak to him. I'll meet you at the hospital in twenty minutes."

"Why—?" Nate had hung up. She pushed End and looked at Oscar. "Why does your master want me there?"

The black lab cocked his head as if to say he had no idea.

"Me either." Madison ruffled his ears.

23

Rafe caught Jeannie's grim expression as she returned from taking the call from headquarters. "What's up?"

"Just updating the captain." She pulled her gloves on and slotted each finger in with undue force. "He sent me this text too." She passed her phone to him.

The text was short but detailed. After a brief scan, one fact stood out. The body from under the ice was Alan Green. A knot of emotion made his chest ache with a new pain for Claire.

"Change of plans. We're taking you to Pleasant Valley PD," Jeannie said.

"Why?" Claire narrowed her eyes at Jeannie.

Claire must have heard the note of tension the detective failed to hide in her voice.

"Something's come up. We're needed there." Jeannie fussed with the zipper on her coat.

"What's happened?" Claire stood and slipped into her jacket.

Jeannie stared straight ahead as she led the way outside. Clearly, she had no more to say on the subject.

"Rafe?" Claire turned her shimmering green eyes on him.

He stopped her before they got to the car and put his hands on her arms. "The body from under the ice is Alan."

125

"You're sure it's him?" she asked quietly.

"Positive." The knot turned to a stabbing pain.

"I'm sorry." Jeannie turned and reached a hand out toward Claire.

"It's okay." Claire brushed her fingers across her cheeks. "I had a feeling the body was his, but hope is a hard thing to let go of."

"I know." Jeannie caught Claire's gaze. "But now we work together to find the jerk who killed him. Right? No more going off on your own."

She locked eyes with the detective for a moment. "Yes, together."

Rafe prayed Claire would stick to those words.

RAFE TWISTED in his seat to catch a glimpse of Claire. She leaned against the door with her eyes closed. Her auburn hair fell around her face in unruly waves, and he yearned to touch it.

The forty-minute drive took more than an hour because blowing snow blocked the road. When they arrived at the station house, Nate was waiting for them.

He nodded to Rafe. "Take Claire to the canteen for a few minutes." He motioned for Jeannie to follow him.

"Is she in trouble because of me? Because she gave me the key?" Her green eyes clouded with concern.

"No. She's okay. Jeannie and Nate used to be partners. They have their own way of dealing with problems between themselves. It'll be okay." At least, he hoped it would. "Let's get a coffee."

"I don't drink coffee. Remember?"

"It's an expression. A coffee for me and a tea for you is harder to say." He led her down the hall toward the canteen.

"How about let's get a hot beverage?"

"Can you hear me using the word beverage?" He let her enter first.

"You have a point." Claire took a few steps and stopped. She made an abrupt U-turn and ran into Rafe. Tears filled her eyes and ran down her cheeks.

"What's wrong?"

"Those police officers. All I could see was Alan in his uniform. He was so proud of being an officer." She leaned against his chest and wept.

He guided her out into the hall, and once out of view of the others, he gathered her in his arms. This was the first of many times she would be hit with the reality of Alan's death. He knew what that felt like.

After several more minutes, Claire drew in a deep, shuttering breath and pushed him away. "Thanks. I'm okay now." She ran the back of her hand under her nose and muttered to herself as she rummaged in her pockets.

"Here." He handed her some napkins he'd stuffed in his coat pocket.

She wiped her face and blew her nose. "I must look a mess."

"All I'll say is if you thought your makeup was waterproof, it's not." Rafe grinned. He wanted to tell her that she was the most beautiful woman in the world and that he loved her, but he knew she wasn't ready to hear those words. Not yet, at least.

"Thanks for that." She glanced around. "Where's a restroom?" She caught a glimpse of his jacket. "Oh, no." She scrubbed at the wet black smear with a napkin, but it only made it worse.

"No problem." Rafe captured her hand in his. "I'll take care of it later." He steered her to the door marked Ladies. "Take your time."

"There you are." Jeannie rounded the corner. "Where's Claire?"

Rafe inclined his head toward the door.

"We're ready for her to make the formal ID of her brother. Do you think she's up to it?"

Claire's crying had been more like a release valve. Not like she was falling apart. Which was good. It meant she had a way of coping and could move forward. "She needs a few minutes to herself, but she's up to it."

"Up for what?" Claire let the door swing shut behind her as she stepped back into the hallway.

"We need you to make a positive identification of Alan's body for the record."

Claire stiffened and moved closer to Rafe. "Will you come with me?"

"Sure." The knot of pain was back in his chest.

The group retraced their steps and took the hallway leading to the autopsy wing. In the viewing room, Rafe stood next to Claire during the process of opening the curtain and folding the sheet back to reveal the face of the corpse.

"Is this your brother, Alan Green?" Jeannie asked.

Claire gripped his hand through it all and squeezed harder as she answered, "Yes."

The assistant medical examiner replaced the sheet and closed the curtain.

She withdrew her hand from his, but he left it within easy reach.

"What happens next?" Claire asked.

"The ME will finish the autopsy, and your brother will be released for burial." Jeannie guided them to her desk and plopped into her chair.

"I hope I didn't get you in trouble with Nate."

"No." Jeannie opened her computer. "But he wants us to join him this evening at his house for dinner and a powwow."

"Did he give a reason?"

"I think he feels out of the loop." Jeannie grimaced. "That would be my fault. Anyway, we need to be there." She looked at them. "I've got work to do. Go home and get some rest. I'll see you later. I think I've got a lead on Tommy Smith."

24

Madison sat in the lobby of the hospital staring at the entrance. Where was he? She glanced at her watch. Nate told her he'd meet her in twenty minutes, and twenty-five had already passed. She crossed her legs and swung her foot.

A tall man in a navy coat strode across the parking lot. She jumped to her feet and hurried to meet him. "You're late."

"Hello to you too." Nate kissed her on the cheek.

"Sorry." She smiled. "But I'd really like to know why you wanted me here in the first place."

"You were there when the guy went into the water. If you hadn't been, he wouldn't be alive." He headed for the elevator.

"What took you so long to get here?" She kept pace with him.

"I was in a meeting with the mayor, and then I had to have a heart-to-heart with Jeannie. I'll tell you about it later." He punched the button for two and turned to her. "By the way, the group is coming for dinner and discussion tonight."

"Great." She raised an eyebrow. "Thanks for giving me so much notice."

"Pizza?"

"We may have to." She stepped out of the elevator and marched down the hall.

An officer stood outside Benjamin Delaney's hospital room. He held up a hand. "The doc's in there. Nobody can go in. Sorry, Captain."

"That's okay."

A moment later, a man wearing a white lab coat pushed through the door. He scribbled something on a paper attached to a clipboard.

"Excuse me, Doctor." Nate flashed his badge. "I'm Captain Zuberi of the Pleasant Valley Police. I'd like to speak to Mr. Delaney. Is he up to it?"

Madison studied the doctor. His name tag was lost in the folds of his lab coat, which hung off his shoulders like he'd lost a lot of weight and hadn't bothered to get a new one. He still wore his gloves, and he had on black combat boots. Weird. None of the doctors she'd ever known wore boots like those.

The man grunted his ascent, plopped the clipboard on the nurse's counter, and stalked off with his back to them.

"Not very personable, is he?" Madison watched him until he pushed through the door down the hall.

"They're all like that," the officer said. "They act like I'm not even here."

Nate stared after the doctor for a long moment. "Let's go in." He opened the door to Ben Delaney's room and motioned for the guard to join them.

Benjamin Delaney lay in a pool of soft light. Shadows filled the rest of the room. Madison walked to the windows and cracked the blinds.

"Mr. Delaney, I'm Police Captain Nate Zuberi." He approached the bed. "How are you?"

Delaney opened his eyes and grasped for Nate. "I ... I ..." His raspy voice barely rose above a whisper.

Nate pulled a chair beside the bed and leaned in. "Take your time."

"No ... time. Alan ... in danger." His face contorted in pain.

Madison shared a look of understanding with Nate. Should he tell the poor man his friend was dead?

Before Nate could respond, Delaney roused. He pulled himself closer, his feverish gaze fixated on Nate's face. "Tell Alan ... *L* is dead." He fell back onto his pillows and clawed at his chest.

"Delaney?" Nate stood.

Red lights flashed on his monitors. "Why aren't they sounding an alarm?" Madison ran from the room. "We need help in here. He's having a heart attack."

"Are you sure?" A nurse rushed into Delaney's room and yanked her phone from her pocket. "Code blue room two-twelve. Code blue room two-twelve." She pointed to the door. "Everybody out."

Madison watched for the doctor they'd seen earlier to return, but he didn't. A different one came running ahead of the crash cart.

"I've got a few questions I'd like answered before we leave," Nate said.

"Me too." Where was the doctor they saw leaving Delaney's room when they arrived? Why hadn't he come when the nurse issued the code blue? Something niggled at the back of her mind. What was she missing?

Half an hour later, the nurse stepped from the room. She crossed to where they stood against the far wall. "He's still alive but in a coma. Somebody turned off the alarms on the machines, and when I find out who, she won't have a job at this hospital any longer if I can help it."

"I may know who is responsible," Nate said. "A doctor was in with your patient when we arrived."

The nurse paled. "A doctor?"

Madison glanced at Nate. He'd noticed something off about the man too. What was it?

. . .

"He signed something and dropped it on the desk." Nate pointed to the nurses' station. "We need to see it."

"Of course." The nurse moved around the station and sorted several clipboards. "This must be it."

A loop and a wavy line filled the box marked signature. No help there. But someone had printed Dr. R. Kimble at the top of the page. Madison sighed. Somehow, she doubted the guy truly shared a name with the character from *The Fugitive*. "Does this signature look familiar?"

The nurse shook her head. "And I don't remember a Dr. Kimble."

"You didn't get a look at him?" Nate asked.

"No. We must have been assisting other patients when he was on the floor." She furrowed her brow. "You think he tried to kill Mr. Delaney?"

"Yes." Nate walked down the hall to the door the phony doctor went through.

Madison followed him. The door led to the stairwell.

Nate returned to the nurse's station. "We'll need any security tapes from this floor and the stairwell."

"You can get those from the office in the basement." The nurse picked up her phone. "I'll call and let them know you're coming."

"Nobody goes into Delaney's room except nurses and doctors, you know. Give the list of names to my officer."

She nodded.

Nate turned to his officer. "I need you to stay outside the room. I'll send a couple others over. One of you stay inside with Delaney at all times. I'll arrange for shifts." He looked at Madison. "Ready?"

She nodded. They walked to the elevator, got in with several other people, and pressed the button for the basement. On the first floor, there was the usual shift as most of the passengers exited and two others entered. Madison and Nate moved to the back. She lowered her gaze and waited for the elevator to stop.

The man in front of her shifted, and Madison saw a pair of black combat boots in front of him. She drew in a breath, grabbed Nate's hand, and put a finger to her lips. He raised his eyebrows in question. She inclined her head toward the man closest to the doors and mouthed, "It's him."

The elevator stopped, and Nate pushed the people in front of them aside. "Police. Let me through."

The man in front bolted to his right with Nate on his heels. A man in a wheelchair tried to stop him but was flung against a wall.

Madison ducked out right behind him. "I'll find security." She wasn't sure Nate heard her, but ...

Following the nurse's directions, Madison raced down the corridor to her left. At the first intersection, she turned right and frantically searched the nameplates. The fourth door on the left said Security. She grabbed the doorknob. It wouldn't open. She knocked.

A uniformed man came around the corner and stopped. "May I help you?" He rested his hand on his gun.

"My husband ..." She gritted her teeth. "Captain Zuberi is chasing a possible murderer and needs your help."

"And you are?"

"His wife, Madison." She pulled her wallet from her purse and stuck her driver's license under his nose. "There. Satisfied? Now, will you please help us?"

"Where is he?" The guard unlocked the door to the security room.

"Somewhere in the basement."

"Down here?" He flipped a couple of switches, and several screens came alive with views of the corridors.

"There." She pointed a shaky finger to the middle screen in the top row. "Where's that?"

"They're headed our way." The guard stood and checked his

weapon. "You wait here."

She removed her coat, sat in his chair, and stared at the screen. The man in the combat boots pulled a gun and shot at Nate. "Lord, no. Please protect him." Her husband ducked into a doorway and returned fire.

The security guard came around the corner and said something to the man. Instead of giving up, he fired again, and the guard fell to one knee. The man lifted him to his feet. Nate rushed forward, but the man shielded himself behind the guard. They moved closer to where Madison watched everything on the monitors.

Too late for her to escape.

25

Madison had been in tough spots before, but this was different. Before, she didn't have the twins. A desire flooded through her—no, not a desire, a purpose—that took her breath away. Her blood didn't run cold with fear of the man with the gun but with the resolution to kill him before he had a chance to harm her or Nate.

She raked her gaze over the modest room. Where could she hide? The low lighting cast shadows in every corner. She chose a spot behind the door. Now for a weapon. She grabbed her purse and rummaged inside. A pen? She put it and her keys in her pocket, but then her hand closed around something even better. She crouched and waited.

Within moments, the door opened.

"My leg ... I can't go ..."

The agony in the guard's voice reached her a split second before he staggered through the door and fell to the floor. His moans fueled the icy heat in her chest.

"Get your feet out of the way." The man kicked the guard's legs and pushed the door shut.

Madison padded across the room and tapped the man on the shoulder. When he jerked around, she took a deep breath, aimed, and closed her eyes before pulling the trigger. The pepper spray found its mark. The man dropped his gun and thrashed around with screams of pain. She fell to her knees.

Some of the spray got on her face. She yanked tissues from her pocket and wiped her eyes, but they still stung. Through her tears, she groped for his gun. She would finish the job.

An arm pulled her up. She punched and scratched, but the man didn't let go.

"Madison, stop. It's me."

The familiar voice broke through the madness. "Nate?" She peered at him through bleary eyes and ran her hands along the lines of his face. The reality of what she'd almost done hit her, and she collapsed.

"I'm here, sweetheart." He guided her to a chair in the hall. "I need help over here. My wife used pepper spray on the man in there, and some of it got on her face."

The nurse lifted her chin. "It's not too bad. We'll take her to emergency and clean her up."

"I'll be there as soon as I can." Nate kissed her on top of her head. "You took twenty years off my life with that stunt."

The cold heat that had possessed her left behind glowing embers of shame. Tears of repentance doubled the tears flowing from her eyes, still stinging from the pepper spray.

"You're a brave woman, Mrs. Zuberi." The nurse handed her a set of scrubs to change into. "You'll need to wash your clothes."

Brave? No, but Madison gave her a brief smile of acknowledgment before slipping into the bathroom. Once changed, she returned to the room. "How's the guard?"

"He'll be fine. The bullet missed any major vessels or bones."

"Good."

"It'll hurt like you-know-what for a while." The nurse picked up a small bottle. "I'm going to irrigate your eyes with water."

Madison lay back on the pillow, covered by a towel, and the nurse went to work.

"That should do it. Here's some salve for your skin."

"How are you?" Nate came through the door. His warm brown eyes sought hers.

She sat up, and a tear coursed down her cheek once more. Did he know he'd stopped her from doing something too awful to think about? When they had a chance to talk, she'd tell him.

"I'll call everyone and cancel tonight," Nate said.

"No, don't. I have a feeling we're very close to a breakthrough. We need to put all the pieces together." She yearned to do something positive. Something that would help her alleviate her self-reproach.

"Okay, but I'll tell them to come later." Nate gave her his jacket. "Yours got sprayed."

"What about you? It's cold out there."

"I'm fine. I'm parked close by, and I have another in the car."

"Wait." She stopped in the hall. "I drove over on my own. What about my car?"

"I gave your keys to two of my officers. They'll deliver your car home later." He held the door for her and pointed to the right. "I'm over there."

She paused to take in a deep breath of the crisp, cold air.

"Madison? You've got my jacket, remember?"

On the drive back home, Madison determined to focus on what they had learned at the hospital. Their visit with Benjamin Delaney didn't supply any new information, but it left her with several more questions. "What do you think Delaney meant when he said *L* is dead?"

"I don't know. As far as we know, Alan's former pals are all still alive. Delaney must know something, or he wouldn't be a target."

"Did you get copies of the security tapes?"

"Yes, as well as a copy of the guy's driver's license." Nate handed her his phone.

Madison pulled up his photo. "Kent Folly. He looks so

young." A fresh stab of guilt pierced her heart. "If you hadn't come in when you did, he'd be dead."

Nate glanced at her. "What do you mean?"

"I was scrambling for his gun when you entered the room." She turned toward her husband, tears flooding her eyes once more. "I would have killed him."

"No, you wouldn't." Nate reached for her hand. "You may have picked up the gun and aimed it at him, but you wouldn't have pulled the trigger."

"How do you know?"

"Because I know you." He pulled into their driveway, stopped, and turned to face her. "You would have seen a man on the floor in pain, and the part of you that is kind and compassionate would have taken over."

"Do you really think so?"

His words rang true with her, but the strong emotion she'd felt scared her. She prayed there never came a time when passion overcame the good in her and she did something she'd regret for the rest of her life.

"Yes." He leaned over and drew her in for a kiss before pulling into the garage. "We don't have much time before the gang arrives."

The pizza delivery van pulled in behind them followed by Rafe with Claire.

"Make that no time." Nate paid for the pizzas, and he and Rafe carried them into the kitchen.

"I need to change." Madison tossed Nate's jacket on the sofa. "Can you set the table?"

"I think we can manage."

She closed her bedroom door and peeled off the hospital scrubs. The lure of warm water cascading over her body was more than she could resist. Let them start without her. She needed to cleanse the day from her skin, and then maybe she could clear it from her heart.

CLAIRE HEARD THE WATER RUNNING, and a prick of envy pierced her like a pin. She sighed and continued folding the paper napkins.

"What?" Rafe asked.

"I could sure do with a hot shower about now." She kept her voice low enough so only he could hear her.

"Go. We'll wait for you."

Madison walked in, showered and wearing clean clothes. She'd pulled her damp hair back in a scrunchie. "I'm sorry to keep you waiting."

Oscar trotted over to her, and she bent to scratch behind his ears.

"We thought you decided to take a nap," Nate said.

"Hah, hah." Madison chose a couple slices of pizza and pulled out a chair.

Claire gave Rafe an oh-well look and stepped over to the counter.

"Iced tea?" Nate asked the group.

"I will." Madison took a bite. "Hmm. Good." She swallowed. "Have I missed anything?"

"No. We decided to eat first and share after." Claire took her plate to the table. "I'm not sure I have much more to contribute. I told Rafe and Jeannie everything about my kidnappers."

Nate cleared his throat. "Did you find anything useful in Alan's safe deposit box?

"I forgot all about that." Claire jumped up and left the room. She returned holding the flash drive. "Anyone got a computer handy?" Excitement surged through her. Now, maybe she'd get some answers.

Madison wiped her hands and retrieved her laptop. She plugged the flash drive in and frowned at the screen. "It's encrypted."

"You're kidding." Claire sat her glass down with a thump. "Alan has never been tech savvy."

"Maybe so, but we'll need a password to open this flash drive. Do you know it?" She hovered the mouse over the icon.

"No." Claire drew her chair closer to Madison. What would make sense to her brother? "Try the date he left the police force."

Madison entered the numbers Claire recited, but the red warning sign popped up on the screen.

"How about his birthday?"

"No." Nate placed a hand over Madison's. "Better to let Randy do this. Eject the drive, and we'll take it to him."

"Tell him to hurry." Claire tilted her head at the piece of plastic in Nate's hand. "That flash drive holds the key to my brother's murder."

26

Claire shook as if a cold wind swirled around her.

Madison glanced at her. "Get one of my sweaters, honey."

Nate brought a thick cardigan and draped it over Claire's shoulders. "I'll make sure it's a top priority."

All those years, and Alan hadn't breathed a word to her. Didn't he trust her? Or weren't they as close as she'd believed? She pulled the sweater tighter around the ache in her chest.

"Between the money we found and the flash drive ..." Nate ran a hand through his hair. "I'm surprised your brother wasn't killed before now. He was sitting on a ticking bomb. Makes me wonder what happened to change things now."

"The letter behind the photo pointed the finger at his friends from the force. One of them must be behind his death."

"Or all of them." Jeannie poured cold coffee into a cup and put it in the microwave. "They could be in it together."

"I'll make a fresh pot." Madison busied herself at the counter. "What about the third friend? Did you find anything out about him, Jeannie?"

"All sign of Tommy Smith disappears shortly after he retired." She scratched her head with her pencil. "Same with his wife."

"I wonder if they got new identities." Claire leaned forward. "Maybe left the country."

"I thought of that," Jeannie said. "I've got Bulldog on it."

Bulldog? Claire looked a question at Rafe.

"Randy. He's the superman of IT at the police department," Rafe said.

"No one can hide from Bulldog." A smile tugged the corners of Madison's mouth upward.

"Not for long anyway."

"But are we any closer to finding who killed my brother?" Claire swept her gaze around the group. "Or tried to kill his friend in the hospital?"

"We caught the man who went after Ben Delaney." Nate passed his phone to Claire. "Does he look familiar to you?"

The bearded man glowered at her from the screen. "Yes." The hair stood up at the nape of her neck. "He's one of the men who kidnapped me—not the driver, the one in back with me." She handed Nate his phone.

"Good. That gives us something to work with when questioning him."

"Before he coded, Delaney said something strange." Madison glanced at Nate. "He said to tell Alan *L* is dead."

"*L* like the *L* in Alan's journal?" Jeannie asked.

"That's the only *L* I know of."

"But we know Begay, Indian Chief, is alive and well. So is Don Irving. He's due in Cincinnati for a rally later this month." Jeannie furrowed her brow. "I thought we decided he was the lawyer."

"We did, but maybe we were wrong. Which would make Tommy Smith the lawyer."

"Maybe that's why I can't find him." Jeannie retrieved her mug from the microwave. "He's dead."

"I don't think so." Claire poured herself more tea. "*L* is in the journal through last month with a checkmark next to his name. I assume that means he paid Alan." She took a drink. "I mean, he may be dead, but it's recent."

"The one who's not in the book for several months is P." Madison shared a look with Claire. "And since Irving probably isn't *L*, he's most likely P."

"Good catch." Jeannie grinned. "If Irving hasn't been paying Alan, then I could see that leading to murder. Alan comes after him for back payments. Irving agrees, but when he shows up, he decides to get rid of Alan and the payments in one blow. So to speak."

"Have you discovered anything else about Irving and the others?" Nate asked Jeannie.

"A little." She thumbed through her notepad. "Begay I told you about. As far as Irving, the other cops who worked with him claimed he was always political. A climber from the start. And he'd swing whichever way the current thinking flowed." She muttered to herself as she ran her pencil down the page. "Tommy Smith was the best interrogator in the precinct. Mainly because he could lie to the perp without giving anything away. He'd tell them their buddy was singing like a canary, and they'd believe him." She looked up. "But, nobody trusted him."

"Maybe *L* stands for liar," Claire said, once again thinking out loud. When the room got quiet, she looked up. "Sorry."

"No. You could be right." Nate tapped his notes. "And P could be politician."

"What did my brother's autopsy show?" Claire shifted her gaze to Nate.

"He'd been shot three times. Most likely a professional with a suppressed weapon."

"He was dead before he went in the water." She made it a statement rather than a question.

"Yes. From the video, we now know it occurred three days before you arrived."

There was nothing Claire could have done. No way she could

have gotten to him in time. "That was the same day Ben Delaney was due to visit him."

"We think that's why your brother opened the door without checking. He thought Delaney was early," Nate said.

"And when Delaney got to the house, my brother was already dead, and the killer was inside searching for the money. Or the flash drive or both." Claire forced her jaw muscles to relax. "He didn't find anything but planned to return for a second search. That's why he tidied up. So no one would be alarmed."

"That may have been what put Delaney in jeopardy." Nate folded his hands on the table. "The murderer couldn't be sure what, if anything, he saw."

"But one of my kidnappers went after Delaney. Did he kill Alan too?" Even though Claire didn't believe that, she couldn't get the image of the big bearded man out of her mind.

"No. I think there's a group involved, and they've been hired by someone else who wants to remain in the background."

"Don Irving?"

"Could be. Or Eugene Begay or Tommy Smith." Nate ran a hand through his hair. "We don't have enough facts yet."

"While I've got you here," Jeannie said. "How about a little help with my other murder, Mathis Thoms?"

"What do you need?" Nate asked.

"A suspect." Jeannie raised a finger. "And a motive." She raised a second finger.

"Have you looked at the wife?" Rafe spoke up for the first time.

"Of course." She glared at him. "Willa Thoms is squeaky clean. Poor woman is undergoing cancer treatments. She's weak as a kitten and relied on Mathis for everything."

"Are you sure she's still taking treatments?" Rafe gave her a puzzled look. "Because I heard she's in remission. Has been for six months."

Claire doodled the name Mathis Thoms on her pad next to Eugene Begay, Don Irving, and Tommy Smith. Such an odd name. She rearranged the letters in his name but came up with nothing. Until ... What if Tommy was really Thomas? She sat up. "I think I may have discovered something."

The group stopped talking and turned toward her.

"I think Mathis Thoms is Tommy Smith." The more she thought about it, the more sense it made. "In fact, I'm sure of it."

Claire wrote the anagram on a fresh sheet of paper and passed it around. Her mind raced through the implications of her discovery. Had Alan known Tommy Smith lived in Pleasant Valley under a new name before he moved here? Somehow, she didn't think so. Could he have just recently found out? Was that why he wanted her to come?

Or did he know his life was in danger?

"That would explain Delaney's comment," Nate said. "He wanted to warn Alan that Tommy Smith was dead."

"Two of the four friends have been murdered." Jeannie shifted in her chair. "Is one of the other two trying to make sure the past doesn't come back to bite him? Or is there a fifth person out to get all four?"

"My money's on your first idea," Rafe said. "Especially Irving. He's the mover. First state representative and who knows where after that."

"I agree." Madison flipped through the journal. "He hasn't made payments to Alan for four months. Maybe he kept putting him off because he knew what was about to happen."

"Possible." Nate stood. "In any case, we've got some direction now." He pointed at Jeannie. "Find out all you can about Mathis

Thoms and see if you can connect him with Tommy Smith. Look more into Don Irving too.”

“Got it, boss.”

“Irving may be behind the murders, but we need the gang carrying out his orders.”

“I’ll reach out to some of my resources.” Rafe gathered cups and took them to the sink.

“Keep it legal.”

“Always.”

“Uh-huh.” Nate raised an eyebrow at him.

“Okay. I’m out of here.” Jeannie shrugged into her heavy coat. “My husband is getting too used to being on his own.” She patted Oscar on the head and gave Madison a quick hug.

Nate yawned. “See you tomorrow.” He put his arm around Madison and steered her down the hall toward their bedroom.

Rafe looked at Claire. “Walk me out?”

His sparkling blue eyes made her blood hum. She rose and walked with him to the door. The living room was in shadow, and he stepped closer. Her heart pounded in her chest as he halted inches from her face.

He lifted her hair off her neck and brushed his lips along her jawline to her mouth. She tilted her head and leaned in for his kiss. Her arms circled his neck as he pulled her against him. She breathed in his familiar scent, and it was as if all the years apart had never happened.

“I’ve missed you.” Rafe’s throaty whisper tickled her ear.

“I’ve missed you too.”

“Seeing you again is an answer to prayer.” His lips brushed her ear.

“Do you really believe in prayer?” She took a step back and placed her hands on his chest. The weight of her question lay between them. Would he understand how important his answer was to her?

He covered her hand with his. “Yes.”

The sincerity in his voice answered both her spoken and unspoken questions, and her love for him surged.

"We don't always get what we pray for, but I believe we always get what's best for us."

"If I never came back into your life, you'd believe that was for the best?"

"It would be hard, but yes." He stroked her cheek. "My one regret is that Alan is dead."

"When my baby brother started having seizures, I prayed constantly." She laid her head on his chest. "My family prayed. My friends prayed. I was sure he'd be healed."

"He was, but not in the way you wanted. David was healed in the best way."

"How can you say that?" She pulled back and probed his eyes for an answer.

"Listen to your heart." He moved her hand from his chest to her own. "Your brother was a strong believer. He's in a place where there's no more pain. No more illness. No more seizures. He's in perfect peace. Isn't that what you want for him?"

"My prayers were answered." Tears flooded her eyes. "In the way that was best for him."

"Yes."

Oscar tapped his way into the living room and made a beeline for Rafe.

Claire chuckled. "You and Oscar have a real bromance going on."

"Get back here, dog." Madison appeared in the doorway wrapped in her robe. "Sorry. He nudged the door open."

"No problem." Rafe gave the dog a final scratch. "We lost track of time." He gave Claire a peck on the cheek. "See you tomorrow."

"Bye." She trailed a hand down his arm as he stepped outside.

"I'm so sorry, Claire," Madison said with a look of distress. "I hope we didn't mess things up for you two."

"You didn't." Claire hugged her new friend. "In fact, things are good. See you in the morning." She had a lot to think about —maybe even pray about.

"I THINK Rafe and Claire are back together." Madison released Oscar's collar and closed the bedroom door behind her. She straightened and was about to speak when she caught sight of Nate with his phone pressed to his ear.

"You're kidding." He paced in front of the window. "Call the funeral home and stop it ASAP." He threw his phone on the bed and rubbed the back of his neck.

"Sounds serious." Madison came up behind him and massaged his shoulders.

"The morgue released Thoms's body this evening to the undertakers for cremation tomorrow."

"That is serious. If he's Tommy Smith—"

"Exactly."

She stopped rubbing. "Willa Thoms would know about his change of name."

"I thought of that." He turned to face her. "And she'd have a big reason to get the whole thing over with quickly. A three hundred-thousand-dollar reason."

"Is that what his life insurance pays out?" Madison sank onto the foot of the bed. "But what difference does that make? It's the same man who's dead."

"The insurance policy is in the name of Mathis Thoms."

28

Oscar greeted Claire as she opened the door from the basement. "Hello, big guy. Where's your mommy?" He trotted ahead of her to the kitchen. The aroma of coffee wafted through the air, but where were the usual mouthwatering smells of eggs and bacon?

Instead of plates and silverware, she found papers covering the table. Madison stood gazing out the window. Claire cleared her throat.

Madison turned with a jerk, splashing coffee from her cup onto her top. "Oh, man." She hustled to the counter, yanked a paper towel off the roll, wet it, and dabbed at the spots. "Good thing it washes out."

"I was trying not to startle you." Claire handed her a dry towel. "Without success." She eyed the table again. "What's with all the notes?"

"There are some questions that keep nagging me. I thought I'd get them down on paper before I forget them."

"Such as?" Claire stepped around the table to read what was on the pages.

"If Mathis Thoms is Tommy Smith, then his wife, Willa,

must know about his name change, and in fact, she must have changed her name too."

"Good point."

"What kind of cancer did she have?" Madison stood next to Claire, absently wiping at her top. "Could she have had it before her name change?"

"Another good point, but why are you concentrating on his wife?"

"She petitioned to get Thoms's body released for cremation, and the morgue complied last night."

"What?" Her scalp prickled with anxiety.

"Nate stopped it in time, but it got me thinking about what she knows." Madison indicated the papers on the table.

It had Claire wondering too.

Oscar woofed and scurried to the door.

"What does a guy have to do to get breakfast around here?" Rafe came up behind them.

"Fix it yourself," Claire said with a grin. "While you're at it, fix some for us too."

"Not before you tell me what's got you two so distracted."

"Questions Madison's trying to figure out. You can help once you've fed us."

"Eggs and bacon coming up." His deep blue eyes glinted with humor and something else that made her tingle. "And a tea for you."

Claire stacked the notes on one end of the table while Madison went to change her top. Rafe placed a steaming cup of tea in front of Claire. When Madison returned, he refilled her coffee cup and sat beside Claire.

"Delicious." Madison licked her lips. "You can be the cook from now on."

"Sorry." Rafe shook his head. "Your kitchen, you're the cook, but I'll help with your questions if I can."

"Good." Madison wiped her hands and reached for her notes.

Claire's phone chimed. "Nate?" Why was he calling her instead of Madison?

"I'm about to interview Kent Folly, the guy who tried to kill Delaney. I got permission for you to sit in. I want you here."

Her gaze flew to Rafe. "Can Rafe come?"

Silence. "He can come, but he'll have to watch from the viewing room."

"Thanks." She pressed End.

"That was Nate?" Madison asked.

"Yes." Claire swiveled her gaze to Madison. "He's interviewing Kent Folly and wants me to come to the station. I asked for Rafe to come along."

Madison paled. "You'd better go. I'll clean up here."

* * *

"DID you notice Madison's reaction when I said I was going to sit in on Folly's interview?" Claire buckled her seatbelt. "I thought she was going to pass out."

"I saw it, but I don't get it." Rafe started the SUV, concern written into the lines of his face. "What are the questions she's talking about?"

"Mostly to do with Willa Thoms and what she knows."

"That's a rabbit hole. We should concentrate on Don Irving and Eugene Begay."

"I agree. One of them has decided to eliminate all connections to whatever happened in the past." She looked out at gray clouds scudding across the sky. They mirrored her inner discontent. "We need to know what's on the flash drive."

"Bulldog and his crew will crack it." Rafe pulled into the parking lot at the police station.

Nate met them in the foyer. "I want both of you to start in the viewing room. I'll give you headphones so you can hear, but only Claire can respond. When I give you the nod, I want you to come into the interview room." He looked intently from Rafe to Claire and back. "Got it?"

They nodded. Nate led them to a medium-sized room with flat-screen monitors and headphones on three tables.

"Claire, you sit here." He pulled out a chair. "Rafe, you're there." He pointed to a spot two seats over. "We'll get started soon."

She laid her purse on the table, fidgeted with her chair, and adjusted the headphones on her head. The only thing she heard was her breath moving in and out of her chest. She stared at the blank monitor. As the minutes passed, nervous anxiety crept over her body. A tap on her shoulder made her jump. She pulled her headphones down around her neck. "What?"

Rafe held out his hand. "Close your eyes."

She took his hand and did as he asked.

"Lord," His voice was soft and soothing. "Guide the interview with Kent Folly and help Claire know when to speak and when to be quiet. When she speaks, give her the right words to say. In Jesus' name, we pray. Amen."

Peace flowed in to replace her anxiety, and she squeezed his hand. "Thanks. I needed that." She turned back to her monitor. The screen lit up with a view of an interrogation room, and she replaced the headphones on her head.

Kent Folly sauntered into the room, wearing an orange jumpsuit. Nate, Jeannie, and another officer followed.

"Please take a seat over there." Nate indicated a chair facing the camera, but it was clear he needn't have bothered. The man knew where he was supposed to sit. He'd done this before.

Claire fiddled with some dials and zoomed in on Folly's face. Too blurry. She backed off a little. Perspiration beaded Folly's upper lip.

Claire backed the view out so she could see all of him once more. He assumed a casual pose, but the slight bounce of his left leg gave him away.

Nate pushed Record and went through the introductions. Claire only half-listened, caught up in the memory of her time in the van. Folly had seemed so young and insecure. Not like a killer. And nothing she saw on the monitor inclined her to change her opinion.

After asking a few questions meant to put Folly at ease, Nate paused to consult his notes. "Mr. Folly, who hired you to kill Benjamin Delaney?"

"Oh no. Wait a minute." Folly started to rise but thought better of it. "Nobody hired me to kill anybody. I don't know what you're talking about."

"We have you on tape. Dressed as a doctor going into Mr. Delaney's hospital room and coming out again. Shortly after which, I arrived to find him having a heart attack."

"It wasn't me. I don't know nothing about no Mr. Delaney."

"It was later determined his heart attack was caused by an injection of potassium chloride into his IV." Nate stared at Folly. "An injection you gave him while you were in his room."

"I tell you, it wasn't me." His Adam's apple rose and fell several times. "I think I'm going to be sick."

Nate nodded at the officer, who grabbed the trashcan and handed it to Folly.

Claire removed her headphones and turned her head away for a few moments. When she glanced at the monitor again, Folly was slumped in his chair with his head in his hands. She replaced her headphones.

"Kent," Nate said in a softer tone. "I chased you around the basement. You had a gun and shot the guard. If you weren't there to kill Delaney, what were you doing in the basement?"

The young man raised his pitiful gaze to Nate. "I was hired to get the security tapes. That's all. I didn't mean to shoot the guard, but he surprised me."

"You were wearing the same shoes as the murderer."

"My black boots? I got those from ..." A look of fear and

understanding dawned on his ashen face. "I think I need a lawyer."

"Don't forget to tell your lawyer we'll be charging you with kidnapping too." Jeannie pointed her files at him and marched over to the door.

Folly's Adam's apple bobbed again. "Wait."

29

———

At the word *lawyer*, Claire raised her hands to remove her headphones, but she hesitated long enough to hear Folly yell, "Wait." She leaned closer to the monitor.

"You never mentioned kidnapping before. That's a federal charge, isn't it?" Folly's leg bounced so much that his entire body shook.

"Yes." Jeannie nodded. "But we can charge you initially and then turn you over to the Feds." She held up the file in her hand. "And they are not going to like the fact you kidnapped one of their own."

"Time to come in." Nate's whisper sounded in Claire's ear.

She yanked off her headphones and left the room. The officer answered the door to the interview room after one knock, and she took a seat.

"Homeland Security Agent Claire Green has entered the room," Nate said for the recording.

"Agent Green, this is Kent Folly. We've been interviewing him in connection with the attempted murder of Benjamin Delaney and other incidents. Now, we are questioning him about your kidnapping. Do you recognize Mr. Folly as one of the men who kidnapped you?"

159

"Yes." Claire studied the young man across from her.

His hair was disheveled from the many times he'd raked his hands through it, and she could make out two red places on his fingers where he'd chewed on his cuticles. He'd let himself be drawn into something sinister, and he got caught. She thought of her brother, Alan. What had he let himself get pulled into? Now, he was dead.

"May I say something?" she asked.

"Sure." Nate glanced at Jeannie, who nodded.

Something about the man tugged at her heart, and she remembered Rafe's prayer before the interview. Was this the time for her to speak?

"Mr. Folly, you have a decision to make that will determine the course of your life. Don't take this lightly. The charges against you are serious, but you have a chance to do something that will set you back on the right track. If you continue like you have been, you'll keep ending up here. Or worse."

She scooted her chair closer. "Cooperate. Tell the police everything you know."

"They'll kill me." He spoke in a low voice as if he and Claire were the only two in the room.

"I wish I could guarantee we could protect you, but that would be a lie. What I can tell you is that we will do our best to ensure your safety, and more importantly, you will feel good about yourself. You will be on the way to changing your life for the better. Isn't that what you really want?"

He held her gaze for a long time. At last, he straightened and looked at Nate. "I don't need a lawyer. I'll tell you what I know."

Claire slowly released her death grip on the arms of her chair. She glanced around to make sure no one had noticed.

"It's my older brother. He works for this man in his factory. One day, his boss offered him a lot of money to grab a woman ..." He nodded at Claire. "... and bring her to him." He bent over with his arms on his legs and his head low.

"We'll need their names," Jeannie said.

"My brother's Lenard Folly. I don't know his boss's name. Len always called him Boss."

"No problem." Nate scratched a note on his pad. "Let's go back to the hospital. You were about to tell us who gave you the boots."

"My brother."

His answer was so faint Claire wasn't sure she heard him right.

"Your brother?" Jeannie asked. "Did he send you in for the tapes while he tried to kill Delaney?"

"No." Kent raised his head. "He's not a killer, but after we botched the kidnapping, his boss said we had to make it right. He told Len I needed to go to the hospital and get the tapes. I was to go at a certain time, and I was to wear those boots."

Claire pressed her lips together to keep from saying what she was thinking. They'd set Kent up as the fall guy for the murder. And they sent him in with a gun, hoping he'd be killed in a firefight.

"How did you plan on getting the tapes?"

"I was going to hide till the guard left and go in and take them."

"How were you going to get in?"

"My brother gave me a passkey. It was supposed to be a simple in-and-out job." Kent raised an arm and let it fall back in his lap. "Nobody was supposed to get hurt."

"So, who do you think dressed like the doctor and injected the potassium chloride into Delaney's IV?"

"The Boss." Kent Folly stared at them with glazed eyes. "And now I am as good as dead."

"Don't say that." Claire couldn't keep silent any longer.

"You have no idea who you're dealing with. He's got people everywhere." Folly straightened. "But you were right. I do feel better about myself. Better than I have in a long time."

Nate closed the file he was holding. "Kent Folly, you're under arrest for the kidnapping of Claire Green and the attempted theft of hospital security footage. This officer will read you your rights." He got to his feet. "We'll hold you in a cell here for as long as we can, and I'll let the Feds know you cooperated with us fully."

"Thank you."

Claire stood. "I'll put in a good word for you too." If she still had a job.

"Before we go, where can we find your brother?" Jeannie asked.

Folly glanced at the clock. "He should be at work. Valley Metal Works in the new industrial park."

RAFE SHUT down the monitor when the officer began to read Folly his rights. He stepped into the hallway as Claire exited the interview room. "Good job." He brushed a hand down her arm.

She shook her head. "He's just a kid. I hated to see him mess up the rest of his life. I only hope he lives long enough to enjoy it."

"We'll do what we can." Nate joined them. "Jeannie and I are heading over to Valley Metal Works to pick up the brother. Can you come back in about an hour?"

"What about the boss?" Rafe asked.

"We'll see what Lenard has to say first."

"Of course." She looked at Rafe. "Do you have somewhere you need to be?"

"Nope. Let's grab some lunch." He helped her with her coat and shrugged into his own.

When he suggested they walk to the Main Street Grill, he hadn't counted on the bone-chilling wind. He burrowed his face into his collar. Good thing Claire had come prepared, or he would have had to give her his coat. The aroma of grilled hamburgers and onions reached them a block away, and they sped up.

"Ah." She paused inside the door and rubbed her hands together. "This is more like it." A Christmas tree greeted them inside the door, decked out in colored lights and ornaments that patrons had brought the owners from all over the world.

He placed a hand on her back and steered her to his favorite booth in the back.

"Hi, Rafe." A waitress wearing reindeer antlers with flashing lights appeared at their table and laid two laminated menus in front of them. "Long time, no see."

"Hi, Peg." Rafe nodded at Claire. "This is my friend, Claire."

"Nice to meet you." She took a pad out of her apron pocket. "What can I get you to drink?"

"I'll have a Pepsi." He looked across the table. "Claire?"

"Iced tea, please."

"You got it."

Rafe pulled his phone out.

"What are you doing?" Claire asked.

"Research on Valley Metal Works." Rafe pulled up their website. "I know about most of the businesses in town, but this one's new."

His eyes snagged on the words under the heading as he read, and his fist clenched. "Well, well."

"What?"

Rafe raised his gaze to Claire. "Valley Metal Works is a division of Begay Fabrications."

"Valley Metal? My brother works there." Peg set their drinks in front of them. "They're all working overtime to make the place spic and span before the big boss comes down from Cleveland next week." She looked around and bent closer. "Don't say anything, but they may be getting a big government contract." She straightened and prepared to take their orders. "Now, what can I get you two to eat?"

30

Claire pointed to something on the menu without really caring. She just wanted the waitress to go away so she could talk to Rafe. But when they were alone, she wasn't sure how to begin. "Begay Fabrications? As in Eugene Begay?"

He nodded.

"We need to call Nate and give him a heads-up." She pulled her phone from her purse.

"He'll figure it out. He's a smart guy." Rafe motioned for her to put it on the table.

"But he may not find out about Begay's visit. Or the possibility of a government contract."

"We can catch him before he interviews Folly when we go back. There's time to deal with that. We need to eat. An army can't move on an empty stomach."

She breathed out a two-note chuckle. "I guess there's some wisdom in that."

Peg brought their food. Claire had ordered a cheeseburger and fries that tasted as delicious as they smelled, but after several bites, her appetite evaporated.

Rafe finished off his bowl of chili, wiped a napkin across his mouth, and leaned back. "You didn't eat much."

"I'm full." She placed a hand on her stomach.

He cocked his head at her. "I get it." He motioned to Peg for the check.

They double-timed it back to the police station, partly because of the cold and partly because snow had started to fall again. Big, fat, wet flakes. Would she ever feel warm again?

"Good. You're back." Nate hurried them down the hall. "Same setup as last time." He opened the door to the viewing room. "Only this time, I want you to let me know if you recognize Lenard Folly as one of your kidnappers as soon as you get a look at him." He handed her the headphones. "You can talk to me through these."

Claire held up a hand. "We need to tell you something before you go in there."

"What?"

"Valley Metal Works is a division of Begay Fabrication."

"I know." He turned to leave.

"And Eugene Begay is coming for a visit," Rafe said.

Nate pivoted on his heel. "I didn't know that. How did you find out?"

"Our waitress heard us talking and said her brother works there. They're working overtime, getting ready for the big boss from Cleveland. She also told us they're getting a big government contract. In confidence, of course."

"I don't know why I bother eating at my desk so I can get caught up on paperwork. It sounds like I need to go to lunch with you two. I'd learn more about what's really going on in town." Nate huffed a laugh. "Thanks."

Claire settled herself at the monitor with an eagerness she hadn't felt the first time. Everything was falling into place. Eugene Begay hired a gang of men to get rid of Alan because her brother knew something about his past that could jeopardize his chances at the government contracts. The first step was to convince Lenard Folly to talk.

But would she recognize him? She didn't get a good look at

the driver, only an impression. Even when the men grabbed her the second time, she was too busy fighting for her freedom to take in his details.

Bushy beard and mustache. Big. Ponytail. A tall man ambled into the interview room and plopped into the seat facing the camera without being told. He kept his head lowered and studied his nails.

"Take off your cap, please," Nate said.

"Why?"

When he looked up, Claire stiffened. She'd seen his face before. He was the intruder Madison filmed.

"Do it." Jeannie's tone left no room for disagreement. "And your sunglasses."

Lenard Folly slid the knit cap from his head, revealing hair drawn back into a ponytail, and removed his sunglasses. The intruder turned into the driver before Claire's eyes.

She keyed the mic. "He's the kidnapper who drove the van, and Nate, he's the intruder who scared Madison too."

"Are you sure?"

"Positive." One more piece of the puzzle clicked into place.

"Your brother already told us the whole story, Mr. Folly," Nate said. "All we need from you are a few details."

"What whole story?" The man drew the words out with a sneer.

"You were hired to kidnap Claire Green, and when you botched the job, your boss sent you on another job—or rather, you sent your brother—to the hospital to steal some security tapes." Nate consulted his notes. "Unfortunately, your brother, Kent, was caught, and you both are facing charges far more serious than kidnapping and attempted theft."

"What do you mean?"

"Murder, Folly. What do you think we mean?" Jeannie's voice came out as a growl.

"Murder?" He straightened. "We didn't have nothing to do with no murder. We were hired—"

"We know what you were hired to do, but did you ever wonder why you were supposed to go in at a certain time, and your brother was to wear certain boots?"

He shook his head.

"The killer was wearing the same boots as your brother, and the guy was murdered on the second floor right before you sent your brother into the hospital." Jeannie pointed a finger at Lenard. "You sent your brother into a set-up, and now we can charge him with attempted murder and you as an accessory."

The big man jumped to his feet. "No."

In the viewing room, Claire jerked in her chair, and Rafe reached for her hand. She squeezed with all her might as memories from her time in the van flooded her mind.

The officer in the interview room raced over to Folly, and Nate and Jeannie shot out of their chairs.

"Sit down, Mr. Folly." Nate stood face-to-face with the upset man for a long moment before Folly complied.

Claire released the breath she'd been holding and relaxed her grip on Rafe's hand. She stared at the tableau before her on the screen.

"You and your brother are in a bad place." Nate scooted his chair closer to Folly. "Your only hope is to tell us who got you into this mess."

"I thought you said Kent told you everything."

"He did, but he didn't know the other guy's name. He said you called him Boss." Nate leaned forward. "Tell me who Boss is, Lenard, and it will go much better for you and your brother."

He dropped his head to his chest. "I want a lawyer."

"Speak up," Jeannie said.

"Lawyer," he boomed.

Nate sat back and sighed. "Interview ended at three zero seven p.m."

"You're making a big mistake, Folly." Jeannie shoved her chair back and got to her feet.

Claire let go of Rafe's hand and keyed the mic. "Can you still ask him about snooping around the rental?"

Nate restarted the tape. "When you talk to your lawyer, you might mention that you're a suspect in another murder."

The big man's head snapped up, his gaze fixed on Nate.

"We found Alan Green's body in the lake."

Lenard opened his mouth to speak but snapped it shut.

Nate stopped the tape again, pushed to his feet, and ushered Jeannie out of the room.

31

Madison sat at the kitchen table with her Bible open in front of her. The verses that normally brought her comfort and peace didn't make sense today. It was as if she no longer knew the meaning of the words.

She closed the book and moved to her recliner. Maybe she needed a nap. Oscar tapped his way into the family room next to her chair and plopped down. "What I probably need is some exercise." She looked out at the lake.

Heavy gray clouds covered the sun. Ice skating didn't seem that appetizing, either. Her gaze fell on the photograph of the twins, and a stab of pain hit her mama nerve. She'd talked to them earlier, and they were having a great time with their grandparents, which she was thankful for, but her arms ached to hold them tight. Even if it was only for a split second before they squirmed free.

Alan's journal pages lay on the table next to her. She picked them up and began to read. His notations followed a pattern in a familiar code, and she flipped through the pages, month after month. "Whoa." She thumbed back a page. This was new. She read the entry aloud. "SC knew? Have *B* check." Was *B* Benjamin Delaney?

She made a note to tell Nate. But who could *SC* be? "Alan, I love puzzles, but you're getting on my last nerve." The *Pink Panther* theme song played from her phone. "Nate, I was just about to call you."

"Is everything okay?"

"Yes. I was reading through Alan's journal again and made another discovery."

"Save it for now. I'm bringing Jeannie, Rafe, and Claire home to dinner with me. Do we have food? Or do I need to pick something up?"

Madison did a quick mental inventory of her refrigerator. "I can pull something together."

"Great. See you in half an hour."

With renewed energy, Madison pushed the foot of the recliner down and headed for the kitchen. Oscar got to his feet and went to his rug by the garage door.

CLAIRE WRENCHED the headphones off and rested her head in her hands. They still had no idea who the Boss was. She'd counted on Lenard Folly to give them his name. Lenard may have been the one who killed her brother, but she wanted the man behind it all, and the Boss would be the next link in the chain.

Nate entered the viewing room. "I need to finish paperwork, and we'll go to my house for dinner. Come on."

Claire rose, and Rafe helped her on with her coat.

"We'll get him," he said in her ear.

She spun to face him. "How can you be so sure?"

"I know here." He tapped his chest over his heart.

For some reason, his words carried the weight of truth, and she believed him. They followed Nate and Jeannie to their desks. After twenty minutes, an officer approached Nate.

"Sir, I thought you'd want to know. Folly's lawyer got them out on bail."

"What?" Nate's face turned red and blotchy with anger. "How did that happen?"

The officer took a step back. "He came in with a signed document from a judge stating they were eligible for bail and posted it. Sir—"

"When did they leave?"

"Soon after you finished with Lenard Folly."

Nate looked at his watch. "Twenty minutes ago."

"Sir." Another officer hurried across the room. "Someone hijacked a car in front of the library."

"Description?"

"Two men. One big with a full beard and mustache. The other slim and shorter."

"The Folly brothers." Nate grabbed his coat. "What kind of car?"

"Gray four-door sedan." The officer read off the plate number.

"Got it. Jeannie, you're with me." Nate pointed at Rafe. "We'll meet you back at my place. Tell Madison plans have changed."

Rafe nodded and pulled his phone from his pocket.

Claire stepped over to a map of Ohio hanging on the far wall. Why steal a car? Where were they headed? A word popped into her mind, and she put her finger on the map.

"What?" Rafe moved beside her.

"They're going to find the boss." She lifted her finger. "They're going to Washington."

"Come on." He took her hand.

"Shouldn't we let Nate and Jeannie know?"

"No time. We'll call them on the way." Rafe jogged to the car. "We need to catch up to the Folly brothers first."

"How are we going to do that?"

"I know a shortcut. Buckle up. The roads won't be cleared."

"Great." She tightened the seat belt across her. The SUV sped off into the late afternoon sun.

Rafe swung the wheel left and pressed the accelerator. The back end swayed on the slush before the tires caught, and they were away again. A curve seemed to catch Rafe by surprise, and the big vehicle skidded toward the ditch. Claire stifled a scream. At the last moment, he swerved onto the snow-covered road and stopped.

"That was close." Claire forced the words out as a whisper.

"Yeah."

After two more turns onto roads worse than the first, the sign for Highway Sixty-Two loomed ahead. Rafe took the on-ramp, and they were on cleared pavement. She relaxed her grip on the handrests.

"Keep an eye out for their car." Rafe pushed the speed of the SUV up a notch.

"It's gray, right?" Claire peered into the gathering gloom. "That's going to be hard to pick out."

"Especially this time of day."

"Slow down. I think I see them." Claire leaned forward and put her hands on the dash. "See the car two up from us? Does the driver have a ponytail?"

"Looks like it." He rooted around in the console and withdrew a knit cap. "Put this on and make sure it covers your hair. I'll try to get closer, but I don't want to spook them."

She tucked her auburn waves under the black cap and slumped in the seat. Her heart beat so fast she thought she'd pass out. Rafe eased the SUV past one of the cars in front.

After a few miles, the truck in front of Rafe slowed to make a right turn. Rafe edged forward behind the gray sedan.

"Is that him?" he asked.

Claire gathered her courage to peek out the windshield. She was sure the driver would be staring in the rearview mirror straight at her, but he wasn't. "That's him. The tag matches too."

"We'll follow them." Rafe dropped back. "Let them lead us to the boss."

"Shouldn't we call Nate and Jeannie now?"

"Go ahead."

Jeannie answered on the first ring.

"We've got them. Rafe and I are following them," Claire said in a low voice.

"What?"

Claire repeated what she said in a normal tone. "We suspected they would head for Washington to confront the boss. We're behind them on Highway Sixty-Two."

"How far out are you?"

Claire looked at Rafe. "How far to Washington?"

"About ten miles."

"Ten mil—"

"I heard him. Keep us posted, and don't do anything until we get there. Understand?"

"Got it." Claire pressed End. "She sounded angry."

"She'll get over it." Rafe eased back some more. "I'm going to let the guy behind me pass."

As dusk descended, drivers turned on their lights. When Lenard Folly did so, his taillights shone two shades of red. Claire smiled at the mismatched taillights. The sedan would be easy to spot in the dark.

"Folly's turning right. I'm going past and turning around." Rafe pulled to the shoulder after the junction. He waited for traffic to thin and made a U-turn. At the crossroads, he made a left and gunned the engine. As soon as they spied the bicolored taillights in the distance, he slowed.

"I'll text Jeannie." Claire moved her eyes between her phone and the odd red lights up ahead. "They're slowing down."

Rafe took his foot off the accelerator.

The headlights swung to the right and disappeared.

32

Claire sat up. Where did the car go? Rafe killed the engine and let the SUV coast to where the sedan turned. A shoveled blacktop drive curved off into the darkness. About a quarter mile up the driveway, two mismatched red lights glowed in the night for a second before going out.

"What do we do now?" Claire whispered as if the brothers might hear her. Although she underwent the same training, she wasn't a field agent. It was one thing to fight for her life against her kidnappers and quite another to rush forward into possible harm.

"We wait for the troops." Rafe flipped the overhead light switch off and opened his door.

"Where are you going?"

"To do some reconnaissance. Wait here." He pulled a balaclava over his head and crept up the drive, a specter in black.

This was the side of him she knew existed but rarely saw. The soldier, the warrior, the protector. She felt safe with him and a little anxious at the same time. Her phone dinged, and she almost dropped it. A text from Jeannie. They were close.

Rafe melted into the shadows. Claire exited the SUV and stared in the direction he'd gone. Her pulse throbbed in her throat. "Lord, please don't let anything happen to him," she whispered. "I love him." The bone-deep chill that had permeated her body all day flowed out of her and was replaced with a peace she hadn't felt for a long time.

A dark-colored car rolled to a stop behind the SUV. Nate and Jeannie slipped out, drew their guns, and came to where she stood.

"Where's Rafe?" Jeannie asked. "I told you guys to wait for us."

"He went for a quick look around. He should be back soon."

"Backup's on the way." Nate checked his gun. "In the meantime, Jeannie and I will move in closer. You stay here."

"No. I'm coming with you." Her stomach churned with a sense of urgency, and she couldn't sit still any longer. "I need a weapon."

Jeannie unstrapped a pistol from her ankle holster. "Here. Now let's go."

They moved with slow, deliberate steps up the drive. Halfway to the house, they heard the furious barking of a dog. Had Rafe been discovered? Adrenaline hit Claire's system, and she fought the urge to run ahead. No loud voices or sounds of disturbance sounded, and the dog stopped.

A moment later, gunshots ruptured the night, and Claire, Nate, and Jeannie charged up the drive.

RAFE GLANCED BACK at the SUV. He prayed Claire would stay put until he could look around and get back to her. For now, he needed to focus on gathering intel. He crouched next to the sedan and listened.

Voices. Arguing. Not close. He crept around the car and caught sight of a barn. The door stood open, and three men were inside. Light spilled out onto the thin layer of snow crosshatched with the prints of men and animals.

A dog barked from inside a kennel attached to the barn.

"Why's he doing that?" Kent Folly stepped to the door and peered out.

"Probably a coon or a possum. We get them all the time." The third man turned. He removed his cap and wiped a hand over his balding head. "Let's get back to your troubles with the police."

"We wouldn't have any troubles with the police if it weren't for you." Lenard poked the balding man in the chest. "You set my brother and me up."

"I was only acting on orders. I had no idea what was going to happen."

"Then why do you have on the boots identical to the ones you made Kent wear?" Lenard stepped closer to the man. "You killed the guy at the hospital and tried to pin it on my brother."

Without breaking eye contact, the man plucked a knife from somewhere and stabbed Lenard in the chest. He yanked it out and stepped back quickly to avoid the blood spray. He dropped the knife and pulled a pistol from his pocket as he did so. Kent froze.

Rafe drew his weapon and rushed forward. "Drop your gun."

The man swiveled and fired.

Rafe dove for the ground, returning fire as he went. He heard a grunt, but the man bolted into the darkness.

"I thought I told you to wait for us." Jeannie ran to him. "Are you hurt?"

"No, but he is." Rafe hopped to his feet and clicked on his flashlight. Spots of crimson marked the man's escape route like dots on a map.

Rafe led the way through the snow-topped weeds, his light trained on the ground. Jeannie followed. The quarter moon shone sporadically as clouds moved across the sky. "He's headed for those trees."

Twenty yards from the stand of trees, a bullet whizzed past Rafe's head. "Down." He swung his light into the trees. A shadow weaved farther into the woods. Rafe aimed and shot with no success.

"Come on." Jeannie ran in a crouch for the line of trees.

They paused to listen. Jeannie motioned Rafe to go left while she circled right.

Rafe shielded his flashlight and placed each foot with care. Patchy snow muffled his steps. After several moments, he stopped. Had the man managed to clear the woods and get away? Rafe took a chance and shined his flashlight ahead into the trees.

Something wet landed on his outstretched hand. In the dim light, the droplet gleamed dark red. Almost black. Blood. Every nerve and muscle in his body prepared for what he was about to do. He dropped the light and lunged to the side.

Bullets slammed into the ground where he'd stood a nanosecond before. He fired up into the tree.

A scream preceded something heavy crashing through the branches. Jeannie arrived in time for the man called boss to land at her feet.

33

Claire stood where light from the house faded into darkness, all her senses alert. What was happening in the woods? She wanted to be there. To help. But she knew if she went into the dark trees now, she could get someone killed or end up dead herself. Or both. A barrage of sharp pops reached her ears, followed by the unmistakable scream of someone in pain. Rafe? Jeannie? She took a step toward the trees.

"Jeannie called." Nate put a hand on her shoulder. "They're okay. Rafe shot the man they were chasing."

She exhaled the tension she'd been holding in. "What can I do to help?"

"Move Rafe's vehicle out of the way so the ambulances can get up the drive. Then come back here to keep an eye on Kent Folly."

She nodded and jogged back to the road. With shaking hands, she started the SUV and drove it several yards ahead. Two ambulances appeared out of nowhere and swung up the drive behind her. When she returned to the house, she met Rafe and Jeannie walking out of the woods. "Is he dead?"

"Close to it." Jeannie pulled off her bloody gloves and put

them into an evidence bag. "With any luck, he'll live to do jail time." She looked at Rafe. "I'll need your gun."

He dropped it in another bag and handed it to her. Jeannie handed the two bags to a waiting officer.

"Here." Claire pulled Jeannie's spare pistol from her coat pocket. "I never fired it."

They turned as the emergency medical personnel approached with the man on a stretcher.

"Why didn't they drive closer to the woods?" Claire asked.

"Afraid of getting stuck." Rafe followed the men to the ambulance.

Claire tagged along to where the EMTs transferred the balding man onto a gurney. She grabbed Rafe's arm. "That's the man from the café. That's the boss."

"Hmm. But who's his boss?"

"I thought we knew." Claire wrinkled her brow at him. "He works at the Metal Works, right? And that's owned by Eugene Begay."

"Yeah." Rafe guided her over to where the police were congregated. "But my gut tells me it's not that simple. It's too obvious."

"The whole factory ownership thing, you mean?"

Rafe nodded. "Begay's been pushed into the spotlight, so we couldn't miss him."

Nate and Jeannie turned toward Rafe and Claire.

"You think someone else shoved Begay into our path to keep us from digging any deeper?" Jeannie scratched her head with her pencil tip.

"Yep."

"The obvious is not always wrong, Rafe," Nate stared into the distance. "You and Claire made the discovery about Valley Metal Works at lunch today. I wouldn't say that was obvious at all."

"Point taken." Rafe ran a hand through his hair.

From the look on his face, Claire knew he wasn't convinced. His instincts were the best she'd ever run into, and she was inclined to think he might be right. But if not Begay, then the only one left was Irving, and nothing had hinted at his involvement in any way.

Nate surveyed the scene. "Looks like they've got everything under control. Let's go back to the house and get something to eat."

"I'm going home." Jeannie yawned. "I'll see you guys in the morning."

OSCAR WOOFED and tapped across the wooden floors toward the door. No tail wag. The doorbell chimed, and Madison put her eye to the peephole. A woman in a long black wool coat stood on the porch, her shoulders hunched against the chill. Something about her was familiar.

Madison cracked open the door. "May I help you?"

"I hope so." The woman shivered. "I'm Willa Thoms. May I come in?"

Madison laid a hand on her dog's head, thankful for his protective presence. What could this woman want? "I'm afraid Nate isn't home, and I'm not sure when he'll be back."

"Actually, I came to talk to you." She rubbed her hands together. "I won't stay long, but it's so cold, and I can't stand for long these days."

Madison opened the door and indicated the chair nearby. She sat opposite her with her hand on Oscar's head. Her visitor had straight brown hair parted in the middle with bangs across her forehead. It didn't look like a wig, but they could be very realistic these days. She removed her gloves to reveal slim hands with manicured nails but no rings. Madison waited for Mrs. Thoms to tell her why she had come.

"It took all my courage to come here, but I didn't know what else to do. As you know, my husband and I own the hardware store in town." She paused and dabbed at her eyes. "I've been sick this past year. And between my medical bills and Mathis having to take off work to take me to doctors, our—my finances are ... well, I have no money. I know it sounds awful, but I was counting on his life insurance to pay off my debt and keep me afloat until I could sell the business."

"That's why you wanted to have your husband's body released."

"Yes. Without the death certificate, I can't apply for his insurance." She brushed tears from her cheeks. "I come to you as a woman and a wife, hoping you will talk to your husband and help him see why this is so important to me. He was a good husband, and I know he wouldn't want me to go through these money troubles if possible."

"Mrs. Thoms, my husband is a dedicated police officer and a loving husband. I'll tell him what you've told me, but the decision isn't entirely his." Madison stood. "He loves and listens to me, but he will not jeopardize his job or a case."

"I understand. All I ask is that you explain to your husband why this is so important to me." She rose and slipped her gloves on. "Thank you for your time."

Madison closed the door behind her. This was a first. She watched as Willa Thoms drove away. In the five years she and Nate had been married, no one had ever tried to get her to influence her husband one way or the other. Something about the woman bothered her. If what Willa Thoms said was true, she could understand her desperation. But what if she had another agenda? How could Madison find out?

The sound of car engines carried through the crisp, cold air. Oscar clamored to his feet, and there was no mistaking who was coming this time. His tail swung back and forth at a fast tempo.

"I guess I'd better warm up the stew." Madison headed for the kitchen.

Nate walked in from the garage. "Hi, sweetheart." Nate kissed her cheek. "Sorry we're late." He took off down the hall to change.

Rafe bent to pet Oscar.

"That smells fantastic." Claire pulled plates from the cupboard.

After washing his hands, Rafe deposited silverware at each place. Nate returned, found a cutting board, and sliced the loaf of French bread. Madison took a moment to watch them and let the warmth of their companionship flow over her. If the twins were sitting in their places at the table, this moment would be perfect. She looked forward to all the stories they would bring back from their trip.

Nate slipped his arm around her waist. "They'll be home soon."

"How did you know I was thinking about them?" She hugged him.

"I know the look." He kissed her. "I miss them too."

"Come on, you two." Rafe groaned. "You're married. You're not supposed to be doing that."

"Oh yeah? Watch this." Nate bent Madison back and gave her a passionate kiss, leaving her breathless.

And Rafe and Claire speechless.

"Okay." Madison broke away from Nate. Where was she? Still feeling the heat of Nate's kiss, she carried the pot of stew to the table. "I want to hear about your day, but first, let me tell you about my visitor."

"I know it wasn't the man who terrorized you the first time because he was with us," Claire sat in what had become her chair.

Madison shook her head. "I'll explain in a minute."

After the blessing, she looked at Nate. "It was Willa Thoms."

"What did she want?"

"She wanted me to talk you into releasing her husband's body. She says they're broke and need the insurance money to pay their debts before she can sell the business."

"Did you believe her?"

Madison took a drink of her iced tea. "I'm not sure. Can you check into their finances?"

"I'll do that tomorrow." Nate made a note on his phone.

Claire wiped her mouth. "It seems awfully manipulative to come talk to you and not go directly to Nate. Like she thought she could play on your sympathy."

"If that's the case, she doesn't know Madison very well." Rafe smirked. "She doesn't even trust me."

"With good reason." Madison raised her eyebrows at him.

"This stew is delicious." Rafe gave her a broad smile.

"Don't try to ..." Madison let her words trail away as she caught sight of her husband. His brows knit together as he stared at his phone.

"Is it the kids?" The food in her stomach soured at the thought. *Please, Lord, not my children.*

He shook his head. "There's been a fire at Begay's Cleveland factory."

34

Claire let her bite of stew fall back into the bowl. "Was anyone hurt?"

"The firefighters pulled Eugene Begay from his office. He has third-degree burns over thirty percent of his body and may not make it." Nate pushed his chair away from the table but remained seated.

"Poor man," Madison said.

"And there goes your suspect." Rafe sighed.

Claire looked at him. He'd said Begay seemed too obvious, and now another one of the original four friends was in a hospital near death. But why? "Only Don Irving is left. Is he the one behind all these killings, or is he the next target?"

"Good question." Nate rubbed the back of his neck. "We need to warn him. And continue to investigate him at the same time."

"Has Randy cracked the code on my brother's flash drive?" Her instincts told her it held the key.

"Unfortunately, Randy had an emergency appendectomy." Nate scooted back to the table. "He returns to work tomorrow, and the flash drive is his first priority." He drained his glass of water. "It's been a long day. Let's finish dinner and call it a night."

Claire chewed a bite of tender beef from the stew. As much as she'd grown to love Nate and Madison, she craved time to herself. Not just a room to herself. She had that here—but space to herself. "I'm very thankful for all you've done for me, but do you think I could move back to Alan's house? I'm used to having my own space."

"I don't see why not." Nate flashed a smile at her. "The forensics crew finished this morning."

"I'll miss seeing you at breakfast." Madison placed a hand on hers.

"You're not getting rid of me that easy. I intend to show up for a few meals." She grinned. "Maybe not breakfast, but lunch or dinner for sure." A tinge of sadness mixed with doubt brushed against her heart. Was she making the right decision? Living here had been like being part of a family again, and she hadn't had that for a long time. "I'll help with the dishes." She rose and collected bowls. "Then I'll pack my things."

WHY DID she feel like crying? She was only going next door. But someday soon, she'd be leaving for good. The tears she'd held off flooded over her eyelids. Claire grabbed a tissue and scrubbed her face.

Her life was elsewhere, and now that her brother was dead, there'd be no reason for her to come to Pleasant Valley. Her tears turned into a deluge, and she plopped onto the bed.

But she had friends here now. She could visit Nate and Madison, and Jeannie and ... She sat up and sniffled.

Rafe appeared in the bedroom doorway. She stood and attempted to wipe away the traces of her pity party, but she knew she looked pathetic.

He looked the same as he did five years ago. The same slim

faded jeans, the same white collared shirt worn untucked, sleeves rolled to his elbows, and the same mussed brownish blond hair over a pair of incredible blue eyes. He crossed to her and took her face in his hands.

"Don't cry," he said in a low voice. "Everything's going to be all right."

And somewhere in the depths of her being, she believed him.

"I'll take your things to the rental." He scanned the room. "Is this it?"

"Yes. If you'll get the suitcases, I can carry the rest." She slung her purse over her shoulder, picked up her computer bag, and led the way up the stairs.

After a round of goodbyes, she and Rafe trudged through what remained of the snow to the rental house.

He came around her and produced a key. "I changed the locks." Once inside, he handed the key to her. "I've got one, and I left one with Madison."

"Thanks."

"You want the suitcases upstairs?"

She nodded. A sense of déjà vu came over her, and she shuddered. Once again, the house felt deserted, but this time she knew why. She moved through the rooms, turning on lights and stopping to bump up the temperature on the thermostat.

"Will you be okay?" Rafe returned. "Want me to stay tonight?"

"Yes, and yes. If that makes any sense." She reached for his hand. "But it's probably not a good idea for you to stay. Not the way I'm feeling right now."

He stepped closer. "And how's that?"

"Very ..." Her pulse quickened. "You're ..." She laid a hand on his chest. His heart beat against her palm. "Vulnerable. Very vulnerable." She dropped her hand and moved away from him.

"You're right. I need to go." He dropped a quick kiss on her cheek. "But someday, things will be different."

She wanted to ask him what he meant by that, but it was late, and she was too tired.

"Goodnight, Claire." Rafe stepped outside and closed the door. "Secure the bolt."

She did as he said and turned to climb the stairs.

FATIGUE HIT HER, and the upstairs bedroom might as well have been on the moon. She would sleep in Alan's bed. After all, it was just a bed. But as she crawled under the covers, the realization she'd never see her brother again broke over her like a rogue wave, and she gave in to the pain.

At some point, her exhaustion must have taken charge, and she slept because the next thing she knew, light filtered through the curtains on the windows. She stumbled to the bathroom and held a cool washcloth against her eyes, swollen from crying and lack of sleep.

In the kitchen, she boiled water for tea and warmed two Pop-Tarts in the toaster. Breakfast of champions. She took her meager meal to the recliner and curled up with one of Alan's soft afghans. Her phone vibrated in her pocket. "Hi."

"I'm coming in."

"No, don't—" She spilled tea in her lap as she pushed the foot down on the recliner. Too late. The front door latch clicked, and a cold breeze raced in.

"Claire?" Rafe tromped partway down the hall. "It's freezing in here. I'm turning the heat up. Where are you?"

"In here." She set her mug on the table and took the soiled afghan to the laundry room.

"Did you sleep in the recliner?"

"No. I was enjoying my breakfast." She returned to the family room, too worn out to keep the note of frustration from her voice, but he didn't seem to hear it. Of course.

"What do you have? I'm starving." He headed for the kitchen. "Pop Tarts? You call that breakfast?"

"It's all I have. All the food Alan bought is gone or spoiled. I need to go to the store."

"We'll go later."

She gripped her mug and took a sip of tea. Was it only last night she wanted him to stay with her so much but was afraid she'd do something she would regret? Funny, she was afraid of what she might do to him right now, but for a different reason entirely.

He grinned, and her frustration melted.

"I'm going back to the recliner and finish my breakfast." She grabbed another afghan and settled herself once more.

"Don't get too comfortable. I came over because Nate and Jeannie are going to Cincinnati to speak to Irving, and I talked him into letting us tag along." Rafe strolled into the family room and took a bite of his toaster pastry.

"When are we leaving?" Shower, hair, make-up, a change of clothes. She'd need at least an hour.

He looked at his watch. "About half an hour."

"Rafe." She jumped up and ran down the hall. "Why didn't you say something right away?"

She took the stairs two at a time.

"Anything I can do to help?" Rafe hollered from the bottom of the staircase.

"You've done enough already. Thanks." Sarcasm laced her words, but she doubted he caught it. She raced through her shower, pulled her clean hair back into a ponytail, slapped on a little mascara and some concealer under her eyes, and yanked on clean clothes in record time.

"Plenty of time." He grinned at her.

She gritted her teeth, shrugged into her parka, and grabbed her purse. "Let's go."

Rafe opened the passenger side car door for her. "We're meeting Nate and Jeannie at Irving's hotel."

"Do we have a name for the boss yet?" Claire buckled her seatbelt.

"Henry Young."

"Have they found any connection to Don Irving yet?"

"No." He tapped the steering wheel with his thumbs.

Another thing that hadn't changed about him over the years. "Something's bothering you. I can tell." Claire waited for him to answer.

"If Irving is getting rid of everyone who knows about his past, you could be next."

"Me? Why me?" Claire stiffened. "I don't know anything about what went on back then."

"You got the flash drive from the lockbox." Rafe cut his eyes to her for a second before returning his focus to the road. "And the flash drive is the last thing he needs to be sure he's in the clear." He slammed his palm on the steering wheel. "And I'm delivering you right to his door."

35

Claire's stomach clenched when Rafe flipped on his right-hand blinker. "What are you doing?"

"Turning around." He took the exit ramp off the highway and stopped at the top.

"No. I want to go. He wouldn't dare try anything with Nate, Jeannie, and you there." Claire gestured across the intersection to the entrance ramp. "Get back on and keep going."

Rafe swiveled in his seat to look at her. "If anything happened to you, I'd never forgive myself."

"Nothing is going to happen." She gave him her most reassuring smile, but her stomach hardened at the thought of all the time she'd be on her own when they got back to Pleasant Valley. Maybe she'd moved out of Madison and Nate's house too soon.

"We need to make sure he knows the police have the flash drive." Rafe checked the rearview mirror for any cars coming up behind him. "Then he'd have no reason to come after you."

"I don't think Nate would go along with that."

"I don't care if he likes it or not."

"Let's see how the interview goes." She placed a hand on his forearm. "Don't do anything rash, please. The idea is to catch him. If it takes him thinking I'm still a threat, so what."

"You could be killed. That's what."

"You can stay with me as my bodyguard." The words were out of her mouth in an instant, and she closed the door on all the reasons why it was a bad idea before she had a chance to change her mind.

They'd reached the city, and Rafe stopped at a light. He turned to look at her. "Are you sure?"

"Of course." She gave what she hoped was a lighthearted shrug. "If he's crazy enough to come after me, we've got him." She peered out the window. "Are we close?"

"A couple of blocks." He wove through stop-and-go traffic for half a mile, then turned into a parking garage. "We'll have to walk from here. You okay with that?"

Claire nodded and got out of the car. When they reached the sidewalk, the wind pushed at her back until they turned left at the next corner. Here, gusts swirled between the tall buildings and tossed scraps of paper and plastic bags high into the air, only to let them dive for the street again. She'd taken her hair from the ponytail, and strands whipped first one side of her face and then the other.

Finally, Rafe placed a hand on her back and steered her through a revolving door into the warmth of a luxurious reception area. The tasteful décor, done in neutral colors, reminded her of hotels she'd stayed at for work conferences. Never on vacation. She couldn't afford such elegant places on her salary.

"Over here." Nate waved at them from across the room.

Jeannie stood by his side. Her stony face and stiff posture made it clear she'd already convicted Irving in her mind.

"How's this going to go?" Rafe asked in a low voice once they were within earshot.

"We're meeting with Irving in his hotel room in about ten minutes. Jeannie and I will ask the questions. If you think of something we need to cover, write it down and pass it to one of us."

"I want you to tell him about the flash drive." Rafe squared off with Nate. "Claire could be in danger. He may think she has it and come after her."

"I get why you want that, and I don't want to put Claire in danger any more than you do." Nate pinched the bridge of his nose. "But I'm not going to do that. First, because we don't know what's on it yet, and second, because it's the only leverage we have."

Rafe stepped closer to Nate.

"Don't," Nate said in a menacing tone. "Or I'll have you arrested. You know I will."

Claire thrust her fists into her jacket pockets. "Rafe." Her words came out in a hoarse whisper. "It'll be okay."

The high color drained from his cheeks, and he eased back.

"I assure you. We'll do everything possible to keep Claire safe." Nate held up a hand, palm out. He glanced at his watch. "Can I trust you in there?"

Rafe gave a curt nod.

"Let's go." Nate turned on his heel and led the way to the elevators.

Claire slid her arm through Rafe's and pulled him close. They were almost the same height, and when she turned to him, the look of longing and concern on his face took her breath away. "I—"

"Are you two coming or not?" Jeannie asked.

He took her hand and stepped into the elevator. Nate punched the button for the top floor, and within thirty seconds, the foursome stepped out onto a plush carpet. Two large men in suits stood on either side of the double door across from them.

"We're here to see Mr. Irving." Nate held out his credentials and motioned for Jeannie to do the same. "These two are with us, Private Investigator Rafe O'Connell and Homeland Security Agent Claire Green."

Claire and Rafe offered their IDs as well. She stared openly at the guards. They didn't look familiar, but she'd make sure she recognized them if they showed up on her doorstep.

"We need your weapons." The bigger guy held out his meaty hand.

"We're law enforcement." Jeannie went toe-to-toe with him. "We don't give up our weapons to anyone. If you don't like it, too bad."

The big guy looked down at her and fidgeted for a second. "What about those two?" He inclined his head toward Claire and Rafe.

"We're not carrying," Rafe said.

"We need to pat you down."

"Fine." He raised his arms, and the shorter, slightly smaller guard did a quick search.

Claire's search was even quicker.

"Okay." The big man opened the door and walked in ahead of them. "Mr. Irving, your visitors are here." He announced who they were and left.

"Great." A man about Rafe's height rose from a couch and came around with his hand extended. "Always glad to meet the men ... and women"—he flashed Jeannie and Claire a smile—"keeping us safe." He waved his arms before clasping his hands together in front of himself. "Please sit. Can I get you anything? Something to drink, perhaps?"

"No, thank you." Nate took a chair across from the couch. Jeannie sat in the one next to him.

Claire and Rafe eased onto the loveseat at the edge of the conversation area. If she hadn't seen some of Irving's campaign brochures, she wouldn't have recognized this man as the same man in the photo from her brother's days on the force.

Besides the fact he'd lost about thirty pounds, his hair was white and obviously cut by an expensive stylist. That wasn't all that cost a lot of money. The shirt and pants he wore with ease also looked high-end. Where had a former police officer obtained that kind of money? Unless it came from whatever Alan had discovered?

"Thanks for taking time to speak with us. I know you've got a busy schedule." Nate pulled a notebook from his pocket.

"No problem. Although, I can't imagine what you could possibly want with me." Irving gave him a practiced smile.

Nate took his time rifling through his notes before returning his attention to Irving. "We're hoping you can help us with two deaths we're investigating."

"You're kidding me, right?" Irving's smile faded. "I don't know anything about any murders. And I've never been to Pleasant Valley. You can ask my campaign manager."

"Who said anything about murder?" Nate let the question hang between them for a moment. "But you're right. The men in question were murdered. As for visiting Pleasant Valley, we don't believe you've ever visited our city, but we will check with your manager. For our report."

Irving reached for his water bottle and took a long drink.

"Have you ever seen this man?" Jeannie handed him a photo of Mathis Thoms.

Irving swallowed and stared at the picture. "He ... no. Sorry." He handed the photo back.

"Well, I'm not surprised. He looks a lot different than he did seven years ago." Jeannie handed him a copy of Alan's photo of the four police officers. "He's the one on your left. Tommy Smith."

Claire leaned forward, anxious to catch the politician's reaction. His forehead creased, and he gnawed on his bottom lip.

"You're sure that other guy is Tommy?"

"Yes."

Claire glanced at Jeannie. How could she say that? All they were going on was Madison's idea about the name anagram.

"I haven't seen or heard from Tommy Smith since we left the force." Irving shifted his gaze to Nate. "That was five years ago."

"What about his wife, Willa?"

"Who? Tommy wasn't married. He had a girlfriend, but her name was Allie." Irving pondered the photo another moment. "You said two deaths. Who's the other one?"

"Alan Green."

Don Irving's head snapped up. "Alan?" Perspiration popped out on his forehead. "How?"

"He was shot, weighed down, and thrown into the lake behind his house."

"This is terrible." Irving dropped the photo on the table and paced the room. "I mean, Tommy is bad, but to have two of my old buddies murdered ..." He swung around and stared straight at Claire. "You're Alan's sister."

36

Claire nodded. In spite of what she said to Rafe before they came here, she felt exposed. What if he pulled a gun? She had nowhere to hide.

He blanched. "We ... I'm so sorry. I'd like to pay my condolences one day if you're free."

Rafe took her hand.

"Thank you." She kept her voice steady despite her brain screaming to run as far away as she could from this man.

"What about Eugene?" Irving sank onto the edge of the sofa cushion, his right leg bouncing uncontrollably.

Nate and Jeannie shared a look. "You haven't heard?"

"No." Irving's voice took on an angry edge. "I told you. I haven't had anything to do with these guys since I retired."

"There was a fire at his factory. He's in the hospital. He may not make it."

The distraught man slumped back on the sofa and covered his face with his hands. He dropped his hands. "I'll have my manager send flowers."

"Mr. Irving." Jeannie tapped her pencil on the coffee table. "Help us out. What do you know about Smith and Green?"

"I don't know what you want from me." He straightened and

ran a hand through his hair. "A lot has happened in five years. Obviously." He gestured at the photo of Mathis Thoms still lying on the table. "I wouldn't have recognized Tommy if he'd shook my hand on the street."

"What was your nickname on the police force?" Jeannie asked.

"My nickname?" He looked at her like she was crazy.

"Yeah. You know. They called Eugene Begay Indian Chief. What did they call you?"

"Politician." He gave a single-note laugh. "I liked to schmooze back then too."

"What about the other two guys?"

"Smith was lawyer. He actually was a lawyer before joining the police. And we called Alan ..." He glanced at Claire. "We called him Hardedge because he was the rule follower of the group. Mr. Law and Order." Irving lowered his head and pinched the bridge of his nose.

Claire's eyes welled up, and she scrambled in her purse for a tissue.

"Detectives," Irving said. "I'm concerned whoever got to the other three will come for me next."

"Why would you think that?" Nate asked. "Did the four of you do something to make someone mad enough to want you all dead? Is that what this is about?"

"No, no. Nothing like that." Irving shrugged. "Well, nothing more than the ordinary stuff. Arrests. Convictions. A little roughing up now and again. You know."

The politician squirmed under Nate's and Jeannie's hard stares.

"Okay, look. There was one thing. But it was a long time ago, and it wasn't that big of a deal." Irving stood and put his hands up, palms out. "I can't go into any details because I promised not to, but there's a slim possibility that all of this"—he swirled his fingers around—"could be related to what happened back then."

"You're going to have to be much more specific than that."

"I can't. You'll need to trust me."

Nate stood and closed his book. Jeannie did the same. Claire and Rafe took the hint and pushed to their feet as well.

"Mr. Irving, until you feel comfortable sharing more details with us, I'm afraid we can't help you. Thank you for your time." Nate gave him a pinched smile and led the way out of the room.

Claire half expected Irving to stop them at the last minute and either confess to the killings or tell them what Alan had over him, Tommy Smith, and Eugene Begay that made them targets for an unknown killer. But that only happened in the movies.

When they reached the ornate lobby again, Nate guided them to a secluded lounge area. A waiter took their orders for three coffees and a hot tea.

"What did you think?" Nate looked at each of them in turn.

"Keeping in mind he stretches the truth for a living," Jeannie said. "I think he really didn't recognize Mathis Thoms as Tommy Smith."

"I agree." Rafe ran a hand over his day-old beard. "He was surprised to hear about Alan's death too."

"Yes. I watched his reaction." Claire wrapped her arms around her waist. "He was upset."

"So can we agree Irving isn't the brains behind the murders of Tommy Smith and your brother?"

"I guess." Jeannie wrinkled her brow. "But where does that leave us?"

The four friends sat lost in their own thoughts until the waitress brought their drinks. Claire wrapped her hands around the warm mug and inhaled the earthy citrus scent of Earl Grey tea. "You can't get this feeling of peace from a cup of coffee."

"Don't be judgmental." Rafe chuckled.

"I'm not." She smirked at him. "Just stating fact."

"All right, kids. Focus." Jeannie gave them the Look and took a sip of her coffee. "The fact is if Irving isn't the killer, then he could be in danger."

"Yes." Nate pulled his phone from his pocket. "I'll make a call to the Cincinnati police."

"What are you going to tell them?" Jeannie asked.

"I'll think of something. The main thing is to try to prevent another murder." Nate stood. "Ready to head back?"

"Sure." Rafe rose and held Claire's coat for her before shrugging into his own jacket.

They crossed the lobby and waited to leave as a man in a gray overcoat and a woman in a long black coat entered through the revolving door. The wind had died down outside, but the temperature still hovered around freezing.

By the time they walked the two blocks back to the garage, Claire's face hurt. She had a knit scarf to wear around her neck and pull up over her nose, but it was back in Chicago. Of course. Time to get a spare.

Back inside the SUV, Rafe turned up the heat and gave Claire his jacket to tuck around her legs. She snuggled into the comfortable front bucket seat, leaned her head against the window, and let her eyes drift closed.

RAFE SHUT off the engine and turned to gaze at Claire. He brushed an auburn wave back behind her ear. "We're home." He liked the sound of that. If only it meant the same thing for both of them. But her home was in Chicago.

She hunched her shoulders. "I slept the whole way?"

"Yep."

"Sorry."

"No problem." He slid out and walked around to open her door. "Madison texted and invited us to lunch. Do you feel up to it?"

"I'm starved, and since I still don't have anything besides Pop-Tarts, my answer is yes."

"Good." He took her hand. "Let's go."

"Are Nate and Jeannie back yet?"

"That's his car in the driveway." Rafe knocked.

Oscar whined on the other side of the door.

"I'm going to teach you how to open the door, you big lug." Madison greeted them with a smile. "Not you. Oscar."

Rafe bent down to greet the excited black lab. "You're such a good boy." He ran his hands down the dog's smooth fur. "Looks like mom gave you a brush." He looked up at Madison.

"I did, and a bath too." She scratched her dog's head. "Now wash your hands. It's time to eat. Jeannie's in the kitchen, and Nate's freshening up."

When they walked into the kitchen, Jeannie had her phone to her ear and was scribbling on her notepad. "Uh-huh. Got it." She raised her chin in greeting. "Whoa. I can't believe it. I was there then and didn't have a clue." She turned a page and wrote a few more words. "Good work. Go ahead and work on other cases for now. You can leave the rest for tomorrow, but thanks for letting me know what you've got so far."

She pressed End and gave them a triumphant look. "We know what they did, and it's unbelievable. No offense, but your brother should have turned these dirtbags in as soon as he found out what was going on."

37

Rafe scowled at Jeannie. What was she thinking? "That can wait. We need to eat." Claire needed to eat. Her already pale face leached of any color. He put an arm around her waist and guided her to a chair.

"I agree." Nate gave Madison a quick hug. "What can I do to help?"

"Pass around the bowls of chili while I cut the cornbread." She smiled at him.

After everyone was seated, Nate said a quick blessing. Rafe couldn't resist looking at Claire through slitted eyelids. This time, she had her head bowed and hands folded. He murmured a special prayer of thanksgiving.

"You've done it again." Rafe licked his lips. "This is delicious."

"Anything tastes better when you're hungry." Madison laughed.

"My mother always told us to accept a compliment with a simple thank you," Claire said. "It shows respect for the person who gave it."

"Your mother was a wise woman, Claire." Madison turned to Rafe. "Thank you."

"Does this mean I have to say you're welcome? I'm not sure I'm up to all this formality. Especially with my sort of sister." He put a hand over his heart and grimaced.

"In your case," Claire grinned at Rafe and Madison. "I think we'll have to make an exception."

"What about me?" Jeannie asked. "Can I be excused too?"

"Oh, man." Claire laughed. "I'm surrounded by heathens. Nate?"

"I'm with you."

"The only two civilized people in the room." She announced.

A smile split Rafe's face. Claire's color was back, and so were her good spirits. The tension he'd been holding slipped away. He glanced at Jeannie. Time to hear what was on the flash drive.

He gathered bowls and carried them to the sink. "Let's clean up before we talk."

"Good idea." Nate stood and picked up the empty bread plate.

Madison shook the placemats over the trash can and replaced them before leaving the room. Jeannie pulled her notes in front of her, and Claire went in search of her bag. After a short while, the friends were all gathered once more around the table with drinks and a way to take notes. All eyes were on Jeannie.

"Bulldog—Randy—broke the code on the flash drive. It was pretty sophisticated." Jeannie scratched her head with her pencil. "He hasn't had a chance to go through all the files on the drive, but he's discovered a lot so far. Like what Smith, Begay, and Irving were involved in back then that made them rich."

"Rich?" Nate asked. "If they were making so much money, why didn't anyone notice?"

"They agreed in the beginning to sit on it—not spend any of it—until they retired. And they used offshore accounts."

"What did they do?" Rafe peered across the table at her. "Rob a bank?"

"No, that would be too risky. What they did was much more sophisticated." Jeannie gave a slow shake of her head as she read her notes. "It started one night when they picked up some high-end call girls. I'm not sure whose idea it was, but one of them said that rather than charge the women, they should make a deal."

"You're not saying what I think you're saying?" Madison's voice was filled with outrage.

"'Fraid so. They provided protection and started getting a percentage of what the girls made each week. And their list of ... employees grew through the years. By the time Alan discovered what was happening, they were making a lot of money. Too much for any of them to be willing to give it up."

"And Alan has proof of all this?" Claire stared at Jeannie. "It's on the flash drive?"

"Yes. There are other files too. Randy's going to go through them tomorrow. One is labeled to you personally. He thought you might want to be there when he opens that one."

"I'll go see him in the morning."

"Can you arrest Irving based on this evidence?" Rafe turned his gaze on Nate. "Now we know he has a motive for the murders."

"I'll have to review what we have first, but probably." Nate nodded, his eyes focused on his notes. "Maybe not for the murders, but for the crimes we have evidence for, and he won't be running for state representative any time soon. I'll have the Cincinnati police pick him up in the morning. He's not going anywhere."

"If all we get him on is running a prostitution ring—even a high-end one—the most he'd get is five years with three years' supervised release and a fine of two hundred and fifty thousand dollars." Jeannie threw her pencil on the table. "That's nothing."

"But it takes him out of action and gives us time to find the evidence we need to charge him with the murders."

Nate's and Jeannie's phones went off at the same time. He cut his eyes to her before grabbing his noise maker.

Rafe's breath snagged on something inside his chest. Both detectives looked like they'd been kicked in their stomachs, which could only mean one thing. Another dead body.

38

The air in the room changed. Even Oscar raised his head from where he was curled on his rug by the door. Claire rubbed her arms against a chill that had nothing to do with the temperature. She studied the detectives' grim faces and waited for them to share what they'd learned.

"There's been an attempt on Don Irving's life. He's on his way to the hospital."

Somewhere inside, Claire knew what Nate would say before he opened his mouth.

"What happened? How?" Madison asked.

"I don't know any details. We're waiting for—" His phone chimed, and he held up a finger as he answered the call. "Zuberi." He stood and went into the family room.

"You don't have any more details?" Rafe looked at Jeannie.

"Not yet. We've asked for video from the hotel lobby, the elevators, and the hall on his floor." She yanked her hair out of her ponytail and redid it with practiced motions. "Hopefully, the perp will be caught on camera."

Nate returned to the kitchen. "He was poisoned. They think it was a woman posing as an agent from the convention center.

She told the guards she was there to go over details of Irving's rally and showed them a legitimate-looking ID."

"Did you get a description?"

"Slim, medium height, blond hair, bangs, glasses. She had a black coat slung over her arm."

"That sounds a lot like Willa Thoms." Madison put a hand to her throat.

"How would you know what Willa Thoms looks like?" Nate turned a perplexed look on her.

"She came to the house. Remember? I told you. She hoped I could influence you to release her husband's body." Madison pointed at Nate's phone. "She fits the description. Except her hair was brown."

"She could have been wearing a wig." Claire touched her hair. "I think Rafe and I may have seen her enter the hotel when we were leaving." She hadn't noticed the blond hair but remembered the long black coat. And something else. What was it?

"You're right." Rafe snapped his fingers. "There was a man ahead of her with a gray overcoat. I assumed they were together."

"What time was this?"

Rafe gave a half shrug. "Around eleven."

"Good. That gives us a time to start looking on the video when it gets here."

"Her heels were clean." Claire blurted out. "I remember thinking she must have been dropped off at the door because there was no way she walked through all that muck without getting it on her shoes."

"So, she may have come by cab or Uber." Nate made another note. "Good catch."

"All the way from Pleasant Valley?" Rafe shook his head. "More likely somebody drove her."

"Maybe she parked somewhere and called a cab or Uber from there," Madison said.

"Could be."

"Hang on. We're not even sure it's Mrs. Thoms yet. We'll know more after we check." Nate retrieved his coat. "Jeannie, we need to get back to the station. The video's coming in." He gave Madison a kiss. "Not sure when I'll be home."

"I know." She stroked his cheek. "Be safe."

"Always."

So many different ways to say "I love you." Claire cut her eyes to Rafe and found his intense gaze on her.

"I've made mint brownies." Madison placed her hands on the table. "Who's going to help me eat them?"

"I was just thinking some chocolate would be good about now." Claire rubbed her stomach. "With a glass of milk?"

"A girl after my own heart." Madison placed the dessert on the table. "Rafe? How about you?"

"Sugar is my middle name." He reached for a plate.

Madison rolled her eyes before retrieving the milk carton and three glasses.

Claire savored the rich chocolate square's hint of refreshing mint flavor and super moist texture. She eyed the pan. Maybe Madison would let her take one home for later. She finished her milk. "That was wonderful."

"Yep." Rafe wiped his mouth with a napkin.

"Thanks." Madison collected the plates. "If you want, you can have a couple to snack on later."

"You read my mind." Claire chuckled.

"How about another cup of coffee before you go?" Madison turned anxious eyes on them.

"I'll take a glass of iced tea." What was going on with her friend? Claire shifted in her chair. "Maybe we could sit in the family room?"

"Of course. These chairs can get a little hard after a while. You two go on in, and I'll bring our drinks out in a minute."

Claire took a seat on the couch, and Rafe sat beside her, leaving the chair for Madison. "What do you think? She's not afraid to be alone, is she? I thought Madison stayed here by herself a lot."

"She does." He glanced at the opening into the kitchen.

"Here you are." Madison handed Claire a glass of tea and Rafe a mug of coffee before carrying her mug to the chair. "Thanks for sticking around." She took a deep breath. "I wanted to talk to you about quitting work after this case is closed."

Rafe choked on his first sip.

Claire patted him on the back. "Are you sure you want to quit?" The memory of her conversation with Rafe in the car not that long ago played in her mind, and Claire couldn't believe her ears.

"Yes." Madison's body sagged. "At least, I think so."

"Why?" Rafe leaned forward.

"After the close call with the man snooping around the rental, I knew I didn't want any part of the action anymore. I've got too much at stake." She turned her gaze to the photo of the twins. "So, what value am I to the company?"

"You've played a big part in finding my brother's killer. You deciphered his journal and done a lot of the research."

"Thanks, but most of our cases don't need research or include puzzles that need to be unscrambled."

Rafe narrowed his eyes at her. "What's the real reason?"

Madison ran her finger around the rim of her mug, and her cheeks took on a rosy color. "You can't say anything to Nate. Promise me."

"We promise."

"I think I'm pregnant again."

"Madison, that's great." The corners of Claire's mouth lifted in a big smile. "But why haven't you told Nate?"

"Because we lost a baby last year, and I want to make sure before I say anything."

"Bad idea, Madison." Rafe shook his head. "He'd want to know. One way or the other. He loves you."

"You're right." Tears welled in her eyes. "I'll tell him tonight."

"As far as the job goes, we'll take you off the payroll as an employee and call you a consultant. How about that?" Rafe tipped the remainder of his coffee into his mouth.

"Okay. We can try that." Madison brushed an arm across her face. "But getting back to what we're investigating right now. Do you think Willa Thoms could be the brains behind these killings? What could be her motive, if any?"

"You've been researching her. What have you found out?"

"There's not much to find. She moved here with her husband five years ago, and they opened the hardware store."

"And we now suspect he was Tommy Smith." Claire rubbed the rim of her glass along her bottom lip before taking a drink.

"Irving told us Smith wasn't married but had a girlfriend, Allie," Rafe said. "Are Willa and Allie the same woman? Makes me wonder if Willa and Mathis were really married."

"That's a good question." Madison went into the kitchen and returned with her pad. "I'll check into it tomorrow. Although, it wouldn't make a difference to her inheritance. If she's named beneficiary, she's due the money."

"Do you think that's all this is about? The insurance money?" Claire shook her head. "Is three hundred thousand dollars worth the risks involved in killing three people just because they know Mathis Thoms' true identity? Seems to me she could have killed him, grabbed the money, and made a new life somewhere else. No one would be the wiser."

"There's got to be more to it. We just haven't discovered what yet."

"I wish there was some way I could get Randy to send me the file Alan left for me." Claire worried her lower lip. "I have a feeling it could help."

"I'll call Jeannie." Rafe punched a number on his phone. After a brief conversation, he hung up. "Randy's going to email you the file. You should be able to open it in Word."

"My computer is at Alan's." She rose. "Let's go over there."

"Bring a thermos of coffee." Rafe cut his eyes to Madison. "And one for me too."

The three friends tromped across the lawns to the rental. Settled at the dining room table, Claire opened the file. Another letter from her brother. That made three in a week. Sadness weighed down her body as she realized this would be the last. "Here, you read it." She pushed the computer in front of Rafe. "I can't."

He cleared his throat and began to read.

"Dear Claire, When I was on the force, I discovered my so-called buddies were running a high-end call girl ring. Instead of turning them over to the authorities, I told them if they'd leave the police force and stop what they were doing, I'd keep my mouth shut. My silence also included monthly payments of five hundred dollars from each of them." Rafe paused. "After that, I knew I couldn't remain on the force either. I called you here because I recently found out they never stopped what they were doing. One or all of them have continued to break the law all this time. It's time to put a stop to it. Unfortunately, that means I'm probably dead, and you'll have to finish what I started. This flash drive contains all you need to prosecute them." Rafe glanced at her before continuing. "I'm so sorry, Claire. Please forgive me. Love Alan."

39

Claire pulled the computer back in front of her and read Alan's letter through again. "They never stopped." That could mean only one thing. Someone still ran the prostitution ring. But who? Tommy Smith was dead. Eugene Begay suffered unspeakable pain from third-degree burns, and Don Irving had been poisoned. That left only one person.

"Where was Willa Mathis going for her cancer treatments?" Rafe asked.

Madison consulted her notes. "Cleveland."

"Why not Cincinnati?" Claire asked. "There are good hospitals there."

Madison raised and dropped her shoulders in an I-have-no-idea gesture. "I'll look into it."

"Could she be the ringleader?" Claire paced around the room, touching books on the shelves and photos on the mantle. How had Alan found out about the continued illicit behavior? Had he narrowed it down at all?

"Why not? She's smart enough." Rafe looked at his watch. "It's getting late. I'm going to the grocery store."

"You can have dinner with us." Madison stood.

"Thanks, but the fridge is empty. And I mean empty. She's out of everything."

"He's upset because all I had were Pop-Tarts for breakfast."

"Ah." Madison gave her a knowing smile. "You can still come for dinner. We may be having chili again. Unless I get ambitious."

"No problem. It was delicious." Claire walked her friend to the door. "See you later."

Rafe kissed her and popped out the door behind Madison. "I won't be long."

Claire pulled her sweater tighter around her. She looked forward to some time alone. A fire in the fireplace, a mug of hot tea, and a good book. She leaned back in the recliner and cracked the cover on an Agatha Christie classic. Alan had collected all of her books. The heat radiating from the fire and the hot liquid soothed her nerves, and soon, her eyelids began to droop.

She woke in a panic. Something soft encircled her neck, and she couldn't breathe. She clawed at the material without success. Adrenaline flooded her system, and her heart pounded faster and faster. Was it a dream? Or was she dying?

"Give me the evidence, and this will all be over." The harsh whisper sounded in her ear.

Evidence? She couldn't think straight. She needed air. The ligature loosened a little. "I ...don't ... know ..." It tightened once more. She flung her hands out, searching for anything. Her mug of tea. She flung it back over her shoulder.

Although no longer hot, the suddenness of the act made him flinch. He released his hold. She worked her fingers under the fabric and yanked it away from her throat. Before he could pull her back, she turned and slid from the chair to her knees, ripping out some of her hair on the way. The room was dark, and his face was in shadow. "Who are you?"

"Give me the evidence your brother has." The voice came in a low growl. "And the money."

"You're too late." Her throat burned with every word. "The police have both the money and the flash drive." She spotted her cell phone resting on the side table.

"You're lying. You went to the bank and got the flash drive."

"I gave it to the police. It's password-protected. I couldn't open it." She lunged for her phone.

The man grabbed her wrist. He dragged her around the table until she was inches from him, the rancid stench of unbrushed teeth wafting over her. Then he snatched the phone from her hand and threw it across the room. "But they will. So there's no reason for me to keep you alive." The gleam of a knife blade glinted in the ambient light coming from the kitchen.

A key sounded in the door from the garage. The man threw her aside and ran for the back sliding glass door.

"Why'd you lock the door?" Rafe flipped on the light. He dropped the plastic bags on the floor and rushed to her. "What's happened?"

"A man." She pointed to the open slider.

Rafe drew his gun and raced outside. He was back in a matter of seconds and helped her into a chair. "He got away. Talk to me."

"I fell asleep and woke up with somebody choking me." She rubbed her neck.

"What did he want?"

"The flash drive and the money."

"He thought you still had both." Rafe narrowed his eyes. "You're sure it was a man? Not Willa Thoms?"

"It was a man. But I don't see how that's possible." All the men were either dead or in the hospital. An idea flitted around the edges of her oxygen-deprived brain. Claire stood. "I'll help you put away the groceries and let's go to Nate and Madison's for dinner. I've got a favor to ask."

"I need to clean up. Will you be okay?"

She nodded. "I'm going to put my gun in my purse."

"Good idea."

While Rafe was in the shower, Claire thought some more about her new theory. It could fit two men. One would be easy to check. The other would be more time-consuming but made more sense. Especially when she threw Willa Thoms into the mix.

"I think we're close to solving this." Claire hunched her shoulders against the wind as she and Rafe trudged across the lawn to Nate and Madison's house.

"Then I guess you'll go back to Chicago."

"I guess." Did he want her to stay? She climbed the steps to the porch and turned to face him. "Do you—"

"Get in here, you two. It's freezing out there." Madison pulled them over the doorstep and slammed the door. "Let me have your coats."

Claire caught Rafe's eyes and mouthed. "Later."

He nodded.

"Is Nate home yet?"

"He's cleaning up."

Claire hung around the door to the hall, and when Nate appeared, she pulled him aside. "I have a favor to ask."

"Name it."

"Will you call the hospital in Cincinnati and make sure Don Irving is still in his room?" She held up her hands to stop his questions. "I know it sounds crazy, but the other favor I want is even crazier."

"Okay." Nate drew out the word. "What is it?"

"Can you get someone in Cleveland to compare the burned man's DNA to Eugene Begay's?"

He cocked his head. "Where are you going with this?"

"I was attacked while Rafe was out getting groceries."

"You were what?" His voice rose along with the color on his neck. "And you didn't think to call the police? You're as bad as Madison."

"I'm fine, and it was over before anything happened. Rafe came back from the store, and the guy ran out." Claire touched her neck. "Anyway. My assailant was a man, and the attack got me thinking. What if one of the men in the group faked his death or faked an attack on himself?"

"Like Begay or Irving, you mean." Nate pressed his lips together. "Come over here."

"I'm fine, really."

He angled her toward the light and examined her neck. "There's bruising along here." He motioned in the air along a line under her jaw. "We need to take a picture of it for the record."

"Okay, but what about my theory?"

"I'm thinking." He took his phone from his pocket. "Hold your hair back." He snapped some photos of her neck. "Next time, call the police."

"I will." Claire held up her wrist, which had turned blue and purple where the man grabbed her.

Nate took some more shots.

She waited for him to finish. "Now, will you please make the calls?"

He punched numbers into his phone and kept his eyes on her. "Hello. This is Captain Nate Zuberi of the Pleasant Valley Police Department. I'm checking on Don Irving. Is there an officer outside his door I could speak to? Yes, I'll wait."

After a brief pause, "Officer, this is Captain Nate Zuberi from the Pleasant Valley Police Department. Would you give me an update on Don Irving?" Nate nodded. "Thank you."

"Ask him to go into his room and check." She gave him a pleading look.

"I know it's crazy, but would you mind checking on him for me?" A moment later, he thanked the man again and pressed End. "Irving is asleep. He's been sleeping all day. No visitors because the Cincinnati police do not allow visitors in a case of attempted murder. Satisfied?"

"What about Begay?"

"He'll have to wait until morning when the lab techs are at work." He raised his eyebrows at her.

"Could you at least leave a request with someone?" She knew she was pushing it, but something inside urged her on.

Nate sighed. "Yes." He dialed the police department in Cleveland and went through his introduction again. But this time, his body tensed. "Chief Rayburn. I didn't mean to disturb you. I planned to leave a message for you to call me tomorrow." Nate listened intently. He lifted his eyes to Claire. "Yes, that's very interesting. When you know more, please call." He pushed End.

A strange, cold excitement filled her whole being.

"They already ran a DNA test, as a matter of course, and they just got the results. The burn victim is not Eugene Begay."

40

"What are you talking about?" Rafe couldn't believe his ears. Begay hadn't been burned in the factory? "You think your attacker was Begay?"

"Yes." Claire sat across from him at the table. "Since Willa didn't attack me, it made sense one of the men involved must have faked his injuries. Which could only be Irving or Begay. Nate called the hospital, and Irving was asleep in his bed. That left Begay."

"Chief Rayburn told me about the DNA results from the burn victim."

"Again, that fits since that's where Willa supposedly went for her cancer treatments." Claire bit her lip. "All the time, she's been meeting up with Begay, and together, they've been running the prostitution ring."

"Until your brother found out and decided to take what he knew to the police." Rafe linked his arms across his broad chest. "Which leaves me with two questions. How'd he find out they were still active? And how'd they find out he was going to turn them in?"

"Once we find Willa Thoms, we should get an answer to both those questions." Nate pulled his coat on. "In light of these new developments, I need to get back to the station." He looked at Rafe and Claire. "Will you two stay with Madison tonight? I'd feel better if you were all together until we pick up Begay and Thoms."

Claire nodded.

"Be glad to." Rafe would have offered even if his friend hadn't asked.

"Be careful." Madison hugged her husband.

"Always." He kissed her. "I'll call as soon as I know anything."

"Did we turn off the gas fireplace?" Claire shot Rafe a look of alarm. The last thing they needed was a fire.

"I'll go check and pick up a few things for us for tonight." He clicked his flashlight on and left. "I'll let Oscar out on my way, Madison."

Claire brought over the dirty bowls for Madison to rinse and place in the dishwasher. "I think your chili was better the second time around."

"Thanks. I—" Madison's phone rang. She rinsed her hands and reached for a towel. "Maybe that's Nate with good news." The sound of the front door opening drew her toward the doorway. "That must be Rafe."

But where was Oscar? Claire placed the bowls in the sink and stepped toward Madison. The front door closed, and the click of the deadbolt reached Claire's ears a moment before Madison's scream.

"Claire, run!"

A loud bang echoed off the walls, and Madison crumbled to the floor. Claire froze. Should she run or try to help her friend? The sight of a gun barrel around the corner settled the question. She'd be of no use to Madison dead.

She ran into the dining room and paused. The shooter could go either way. She was trapped in a deadly game of ring-around-the-rosy. She ducked down and crept toward the family/living room doorway. Could she make it out the front door without getting a bullet in the back?

"I know you're there, Claire. I can hear you breathing. Any way you go, I'll get to you. Meanwhile, your friend is bleeding to death."

The woman's sing-song voice sent a chill through her. "What do you want, Willa?"

"Good for you. You figured it out. I want you dead, witch. You spoiled everything."

"I didn't gather the information. Alan did." Where was Rafe? Didn't he hear Oscar's frantic barking at the back door? "So why me?"

"If you're trying to keep me talking, don't bother. Your boyfriend is having a nice long nap next door."

Fear threatened to take over Claire's mind. She frantically scanned the room. What could she use as a weapon? "You didn't answer my question."

"If you hadn't come to visit, they wouldn't have found his body until the spring thaw. By then, we would have been long gone."

"We?"

A thump against a kitchen chair. Claire tossed a pinecone from the dining room centerpiece across the living room toward the stairs leading to the basement. She was rewarded by footsteps headed for the doorway from the hall into the family room. It was cutting it close. She prayed Madison's gun was where she always kept it.

Claire raced across the kitchen and yanked the drawer open. She grabbed the pistol and whirled. Willa rushed into the kitchen, her weapon aimed at Claire. Both guns fired at the same time. The women stared at each other for a moment before Willa's gun fell from her hand, and she slid to the floor.

Claire's entire body shook. She laid Madison's gun on the table and dropped into a chair. Sirens split the air, but they barely registered with her until men and women in uniform filled the house. It was the EMTs around Madison that brought Claire to her senses. "She's pregnant."

"Got it."

"What did you say?" Nate took her by the arms and yanked her out of her chair. "Madison's pregnant?"

41

"She didn't want to disappoint you if ..." Claire's heart broke at the pain in his face. "She planned on telling you tonight."

He let go of her. "I'm sorry." He gazed after the gurney carrying his wife. "I need to go."

Claire sank back into her chair and lowered her head into her arms. *Lord, take care of Madison and her baby, and Nate. And Rafe.*

"Claire." Rafe kneeled beside her. "I ..." His face was etched with regret. "Are you okay?"

"Is Willa dead?" The gun in her hand, the explosion, and the woman falling to the floor replayed in her mind over and over again.

"She was alive when they took her away." He sat beside her and took her hands in his. "First time?"

She nodded. Her stomach knotted, and she rushed to the sink.

"First time's rough, but truth is, it's never easy." Rafe pulled her hair back behind her ears.

"I never want to have to do that again." Claire tore off a paper towel and wiped her mouth.

"But thank God you did." He turned her to look at him. "She

would have killed you, Madison, and who knows how many others."

"I pray she lives." She wrapped her arms around Rafe.

"Me too. For your sake and hers." He kissed the top of her head.

"Claire, are you okay?" Jeannie rushed into the room. "Nate told me what happened."

She disengaged from Rafe and nodded at Jeannie.

"I need to bag the guns and take your statement if you're up to it."

"Will you stay with me?" Claire looked at Rafe.

"I'm not going anywhere." He pulled out chairs for the women. "Let me get Oscar from the screened porch and put him in one of the kid's bedrooms."

When he returned, he took a seat next to Claire.

"I'm glad you're here." Jeannie pulled her notebook out of her purse along with a pencil. "I'll need your statement too."

Claire held Rafe's hand as she related her account of what happened to Jeannie. When she reached the part about grabbing Madison's gun and shooting Willa, she squeezed so hard he gave a small grunt. She eased her hold.

"As for you ..." Jeannie peered at Rafe over the rim of her glasses. "I'm curious about how she got the drop on you."

"She must have been in the house when I got there. When I came in to turn off the fireplace, she came from behind and stabbed me with a syringe." He rubbed the red spot on his neck. "I don't remember anything after that."

"I guess she thought we'd return to the rental house after dinner, so she waited there." Claire rubbed her arms. "She said I ruined everything, but Madison would have noticed that Alan wasn't around, and she and Nate would have looked for him."

"You can't pay any attention to her." Jeannie closed her notebook. "She needs to blame someone for what went wrong with her plans, and you were as good as anybody."

"If she'd just disappeared, she could have been off somewhere enjoying the money from her offshore bank account."

"Unless she can't get to the money," Rafe said. "Begay could have set up the account, so he's the only one who can access it."

"That's all for now." Jeannie stood. "I want you two to go somewhere other than the rental or here for a while. Forensics needs to go over both houses. But let me know where you are."

"We can go to my aunt and uncle's house next door. I'm house-sitting while they're away." Rafe held Claire's coat for her.

"Good." Jeannie shouldered her purse.

Claire didn't move.

"What's up?" Rafe asked.

"I want to go to the hospital." Claire fought to keep her voice calm and assertive.

"I don't think that's a good idea." Jeannie shared a look with Rafe. "You've been through a lot in the last few hours. You need rest."

"Either you take me ..." She looked at Rafe. "Or I'll drive myself. Either way, I'm going." She did need to rest, but not until she'd seen Madison. And Willa Thoms.

"Madison's probably still in surgery." Rafe rubbed his brow as if trying to smooth away a headache. "And if she's out, I doubt we can get in to see her tonight."

"Maybe. But at least we can be there to support Nate." She let her own pain and vulnerability spill onto her face for him to see. "I know what it's like to have someone you love hurting."

Rafe pulled her to him and held her for a moment before letting her go. "You're right. We should be there."

Twenty minutes later, they pulled into a parking space at the hospital. Claire jumped out of the SUV and quickly headed for the main doors.

"Slow down." Rafe caught her arm. "You come in at a run, and the woman at the information desk is likely to call security on you."

She took his hand and matched her steps to his. "Is that better?"

He grunted a yes.

"I called ahead. She's in room two seventeen." Claire scanned the lobby for the elevator sign. She found herself saying the same prayer over and over. *Let Madison and the baby be fine, and let Willa be alive.* She cut her eyes to Rafe. He knew she wanted to be near Madison and support Nate, but she hadn't said anything about Willa.

"This way." Rafe put a hand on her back. In the elevator, he reached for her hand once more. "She'll be okay."

But he wasn't there. He didn't hear Madison's cry or see her collapse on the floor. Claire's pulse beat in her throat. The shot was so close. How could the bullet have missed the baby?

"You're shaking." Rafe turned to her as the elevator stopped and the doors opened.

"I'm fine." She tugged him off into the hallway. "I'm a little cold."

Madison's room was near the nurse's station. Rafe knocked and opened the door. Nate got up from a chair by the window. His dark hair was furrowed from all the times he'd plowed his fingers through it, and a shadow of whiskers covered his chin and jawline.

"Any news?" Rafe asked.

"Not yet." Nate pulled chairs around for them. "The docs called and let me know she's doing okay during the surgery, but nothing about ..." He put his face in his hands.

Nate's pain filled the room, and Claire couldn't catch her breath. Maybe she'd made a mistake. Maybe they shouldn't have come. If only she hadn't told the EMTs about the baby. Nate wouldn't have overheard, and he wouldn't be in so much agony now. But how could she not tell them?

The door burst open, and a white-coated man strode over to Nate. "Captain Zuberi."

Nate started to rise.

"Don't get up." The doctor put a hand on his shoulder.

42

Claire leaped to her feet as soon as she caught sight of the doctor. He paid no attention to her. His entire focus was on Nate. Did that mean he had good news or bad news? She wanted to scream, "Out with it," but managed to hold her tongue. However, when the doctor kept Nate seated, her knees weakened, and she dropped into her chair again.

"Your wife is in recovery," the doctor said. "We got the bullet. It was lodged in a rib on her left side. A little lower, and it would have hit her heart. We were able to perform the surgery with minimal anesthesia since it wasn't deep." He pulled off his paper hat, exposing a head of thinning blond hair. "Forgot I had that on. Anyway. She'll be sore for a while."

And the baby? Claire held her breath. What about her baby?

"Our baby?" Nate's glistening eyes focused on the doctor's face.

"We believe your baby should be fine. But the next few days will be critical. We want your wife on complete bed rest for three days. Make an appointment with her obstetrician and follow his instructions after that. Anything else?"

"I don't think so."

"Will she come back to this room from recovery?" Rafe asked.

"Yes, but I'm leaving orders to limit the number of visitors for a day so she can rest." He eyed Rafe. "Are you family?"

"Her brother."

Claire averted her eyes. It was only a little lie.

"This is my wife." He put his arm around her shoulders.

And that was a big one. Claire forced a smile.

"Okay. You can see her, but limit it to five minutes every two hours." He gave them a stern look. "Rest is the key."

"Got it."

Claire waited for the soft swoosh of the door closing before rounding on Rafe. "Why did you have to drag me into your lies?"

"You want to see Madison?" He met her indignant look with one of his own.

She did, but she hated lying to do so. Nate remained slumped in his chair, head down, oblivious to what was happening around him.

"Is there a public bathroom on this floor?" she asked.

"Out the door and to the left. About halfway to the elevators." Rafe snatched her hand as she passed. "Sorry."

"Me too." She laid a hand on his chest. "I know your heart was in the right place." She opened the door and pointed left. "That way?"

Rafe nodded.

As she returned, she surveyed the hall. The nurse's desk stood across from Madison's room. Farther down, a male police officer sat outside a door. "Wonder if that's Willa Thom's room," she murmured under her breath.

A woman screamed, and a man dressed in black rushed from a room at the end of the hall. He yanked open the door to the stairway.

"Stop. Police." The officer jumped up and sprinted after him.

Moments later, a big, bearded man pushed the stairwell door

open and hurried across the hall into the room where the police officer had been stationed.

Was that who she thought it was? Her heart pounded in her chest. He had to be stopped. She took a step toward the room.

Rafe poked his head out of Madison's door. "What's all the racket?" He scanned the hallway.

"Eugene Begay." Claire grabbed his arm. "He's in a room down the hall. We have to stop him before he hurts someone else."

"BEGAY'S HERE?" Rafe turned Claire to face him. "Are you sure?"

She nodded. Rafe broke into a jog, aware she was right behind him.

The police officer returned from the stairwell and crossed to Begay's room.

"Stop," Rafe called out to him.

But he was too late. Angry voices reached them a second before the crash and thud of something hard hitting the wall.

The door to the room flew open, smashing Rafe in the side of the head. Claire caught him as he staggered back, and for a moment, he forgot where he was. The sight of Begay escaping down the stairs stirred him to action, and like a bull enraged by a red cape, Rafe charged after the fleeing figure.

What he lacked in size, Rafe made up for in agility. He raced down the stairs, gaining steadily on the big man. By the time they reached the bottom, he was within inches of grabbing Begay by the collar.

The door opened, and a guard pointed his gun at Begay. "Stop, or I'll shoot."

Rafe dove onto Begay's broad back. As the big man wrestled the weapon from the guard's grip, the gun went off, and the three men tumbled into the snow-covered bushes. Rafe clung to Begay, but the guard fell away from the tangle of arms and legs.

Begay stood and, with a roar, shook Rafe off his back like an old coat.

Rafe bounced to his feet in time to see the big man loping toward the parking lot. He turned to the guard. "You need help?"

Blood ran down the right side of the guard's face. "I think it took off part of my ear." He grimaced and pressed his shirt sleeve to the side of his head. "I can call for help. Don't let the jerk get away."

Rafe sprinted to where he'd parked his SUV near the exit, stood on the bumper, and watched for movement. There. A white sedan rolled through the aisles headed his way. He got in and started his engine.

The sedan gained speed as it approached the exit. Rafe hit the accelerator. The two vehicles collided with a loud bang that echoed off the parked cars. Begay's sedan spun around before coming to rest, its front end against the SUV.

Rafe leaped out and pulled his gun. "Hands up, Begay." As he rounded the back of the crumpled white car, the big man pulled himself out of the driver's seat and turned.

"You're no cop." He raised a meaty fist wrapped around the gun he'd taken from the officer in the hospital and sneered at Rafe.

WHEN RAFE TOOK off after Begay, Claire rushed into the hospital room Begay had just exited. The young officer lay sprawled on the floor, unconscious. She pressed her fingers to his neck and was rewarded with a pulse. Now to get help.

The hallway was packed with guards, police, and nurses. Nate stood at the center of one group. When he saw her emerge from the room, he hurried over. "What were you doing in there?"

"Your officer needs help." She gestured over her shoulder. "He's been knocked out."

He turned from her and called into the crowd. "We need a nurse in room two twenty ASAP."

Two nurses scooted past them. Nate turned back to her. "What happened to him, and where's Rafe?"

"Begay distracted the officer and snuck into the room. When the officer returned, he and Begay fought. Begay left, and Rafe ran after him. I don't know—"

"He went after Begay on his own? The idiot." Nate checked his weapon. "Which way did they go?"

"Down the stairs." Claire watched as Nate raced off. What now? She glanced at the room she'd just come from. This might be her only chance to discover how Willa Thoms was doing.

43

Rafe stared at the gun in the big man's hand. He always knew a day like this would come. Only why'd it have to be now? "I'm undercover."

Begay shook his head. "I don't believe you."

"You're right. He's not a cop." Nate appeared behind Begay and put the barrel of his gun against his temple. "But I am. Give me the gun."

Begay dropped his arm as if in submission. Without warning, he swung his arm up and back in an arc, catching Nate off guard. A shot rang out as Nate fired but missed.

Rafe holstered his gun, afraid he could hit Nate. Instead, he ran at Begay. With every ounce of power he had, he side-kicked the big man's right knee. Begay buckled in pain but still tried to aim his gun at Rafe. Another kick to his arm sent the gun flying.

The next kick was meant for his head. But Begay held up his hands in surrender.

"No more." He slumped to the ground. "I think you broke my kneecap."

Rafe bent to catch his breath.

Nate came beside him. "You all right?"

"I need to hit the gym more."

"You and me both, buddy." Nate patted him on the back.

Noise filled the air as officers tumbled from police cars and all yelled at once. Rafe stepped away from the chaos. His phone rang.

NO ONE PAID any attention to her. Claire slipped into the room. The two nurses bent over the police officer, who was now awake and answering their questions. A wave of relief swept through her. At least Begay hadn't left another victim in his wake. She glided across the floor to the side of the bed.

She looked down and stifled a cry of surprise. The person in the bed was not Willa Thoms. It was a man.

One of the nurses spun around. "Excuse me. No one is allowed in here. Come with me."

"I'm part of the investigation."

"We'll see about that." She grabbed Claire's arm and marched her out the door. "Do any of you know this woman?"

Jeannie looked up from her notebook. "It's okay. She's with me."

"Please tell her not to enter the patient's room without permission." The nurse huffed away.

"You heard her." Jeannie waggled her eyebrows at her. "No more messing with the patients."

"I wasn't. I thought that was Willa Thoms' room." Claire rubbed her arms. "I only wanted to find out if she was okay."

"Thoms is on the third floor." Jeannie inclined her head toward the room. "That's Delaney."

"Ben Delaney. Of course." No wonder Begay was after him. "Tell the nurses to check their patient right away. I think Begay went in to kill him. I'm not sure whether or not the officer was able to stop him."

Jeannie hurried into the room.

Claire paced the hall, waiting for her return. Delaney was the key witness. He had information that could convict Begay of murder. And Willa Thoms as his accomplice. Even without his testimony, both would be charged with assault and attempted murder, besides all the crimes related to their prostitution ring. That should earn them lots of years behind bars.

But it would feel good to put them away for her brother's murder, and only Delaney could help her do that.

"He's okay," Jeannie said. "And he's showing signs of coming out of his coma."

"Good." Maybe there was power in prayer. Now if only he remembered everything that happened.

"Where are Nate and Rafe?"

"Chasing Eugene Begay." She related what she knew to Jeannie.

The detective phoned for backup in the parking lot. "You call Rafe. I'll try Nate."

Claire pressed numbers on her phone. No answer. She tried again. Still no answer. One more time, and she'd go down there herself.

"Hi." His weary voice sounded miles away.

"Thought I'd check to see if you were still alive." Tears threatened to overwhelm her, and she worked to keep her tone light.

"Barely." He sighed. "That guy is a monster."

"But I'm assuming you've got him in custody?"

"Oh yeah. It took extra, extra-large zip ties for his wrists." Rafe uttered a mirthless laugh. "Course, before we take him to jail, he has to be looked at by a doc."

"Why? What did you do?"

"I tapped him on the knee. Just enough to throw him off balance."

"Sure, you did." Claire covered her face with her hand and shook her head.

"Now he's claiming his knee's broken. Can you believe it? You should see this guy."

"I have, and I know you." Claire let a little bite into her tone. "But I also know that whatever you did was done in self-defense and to protect Nate. How is he, by the way?"

"He's fine. We're headed your way now. See you soon."

Claire's energy drained away as if a plug had been pulled inside her, and her stomach sent nagging messages to her brain about low fuel. She caught the attention of a nearby nurse. "Is there any food on this floor?"

"We have some snacks and drinks in the alcove there." The nurse pointed to her left.

"Hey." Claire snagged Jeannie as she passed. "I'm going back to Madison's room if you need me."

Jeannie nodded and returned to what she was doing.

In the small room off the hall, Claire sorted through the chips and energy bars. She chose a couple that looked good, grabbed a soft drink, and headed down the hall. Part of her was disappointed to see the empty bed, but another part breathed a sigh of relief that Madison hadn't returned from recovery. Maybe she could get some time to herself.

Once settled in the recliner, she popped the top on the canned soda and took a swig. That was better. Just as her eyes closed, the door to the hospital room burst open.

"Delaney's ready to talk." Jeannie hurried in. "Want to come?"

Claire levered herself upright and followed the detective down the hall.

At the door to Delaney's room, Jeannie put an arm up to block Claire. "Inside, you watch and listen. No talking. No asking questions. Got it?"

"But—"

"No buts." Jeannie shook her head.

"Okay." Claire let her face sag with disappointment.

"Forget it. Your sad look won't work with me." Jeannie swiveled and pushed through the door.

Claire followed her into Delaney's room. A nurse stopped fussing with his pillows and gave them a stern look.

"Fifteen minutes. No more," she said in a tone used to being obeyed.

Had Jeannie met her match?

"Yes, ma'am." Jeannie pulled a chair close to the bed and motioned for Claire to do the same. Jeannie watched as the nurse left, and after the door whooshed shut, she turned her attention to the man propped up in bed. "Hello, Mr. Delaney. I'm Detective Jeannie Jansen, and this is Homeland Security Agent Clair Green."

He swung his gaze to Claire. "You're Alan's sister."

She smiled at him and nodded.

Tears welled in his eyes. "Am I too late? Is he dead?"

"I'm afraid so." Claire touched his hand.

He laid his head back and closed his eyes. Sadness clouded his features.

"You couldn't have saved him. He was dead before you got to the house."

His eyes popped open. "How do you know?"

"We saw you on the security cameras." Jeannie shot a time-to-step-back look at Claire. "We also saw the guy who took Mr. Green." She scooted closer. "What can you tell me about Mr. Green and what happened during his time on the police force?"

"He had three close friends. Men he trusted with his life."

"Eugene Begay, Don Irving, and Tommy Smith. We know about them." Jeannie nodded, encouraging him to continue.

"Things were good until he found evidence they'd been running a protection racket for call girls and, later, running the girls on their own." Delaney sighed. "That's when Alan realized he couldn't be friends with them anymore and determined he had to stop them."

"Is that when he confronted them, and they left the force?"

"Yes. He hired me to communicate with each of them and

keep tabs on them. I reported to him every month and brought ...” Delaney cut his eyes to Claire.

“We know about the monthly payouts,” Jeannie said.

Delaney shifted his gaze between Jeannie and Claire. “He didn’t spend any of the money. He was leaving it for Claire to give to charity.”

“Yeah. He left a letter for her.” Jeannie pressed her lips together. “How did you know Smith was dead?”

“I went by the hardware store and saw the police outside. It wasn’t hard to strike up a conversation. I flashed my retirement ID from the Chicago force, and the officer outside told me about the scene inside.”

Claire looked at Jeannie. An officer was about to get into trouble somewhere in Pleasant Valley.

“You guessed he was dead?”

“I knew it in my gut. And I had a pretty good idea who did it.”

“Who?”

“His wife, Allie. It wouldn’t be the first time she’s killed someone.”

“Who else has she murdered?” Jeannie stared at Delaney, her pencil poised over her notepad.

“Her sister Willa.”

44

"Willa?" Claire couldn't contain her shock. "Did she take her sister's identification when Tommy Smith became Mathis Thoms?"

Jeannie furrowed her brow at Claire's outburst.

"Before that. As far as the family knows, Allie died that day, not Willa."

"Do they still—"

"Back to Smith's murder." Jeannie sliced through Claire's next question in a take-charge tone. "Eugene Begay swears he did it."

"He would. He's crazy about her." Delaney shifted in the bed. "Could you hand me that water?"

"Sure." Jeannie gave him the Styrofoam cup with a straw and waited for him to take a drink.

"Thanks." He wiped a hand across his mouth. "Begay was one of her clients."

"Allie was a call girl?" A look of surprise swept across Jeannie's face.

He nodded. "And she ran the business after the guys retired from the force."

"Was Tommy Smith one of her clients too?"

"Yes, but he married her."

"Did he know about Begay? Or that she and Begay were still in business together?"

"Nope. At least not until recently." Delaney yawned. "When Tommy found out, he contacted me, and I told Alan." He looked once more at Claire. "That's why your brother called you. He decided to blow the whistle on them. For all of it. The protection racket, the prostitution ring, the whole thing."

"And he ended up putting a very big target on his back." Anger spiraled from the pit of Claire's stomach.

"I'll miss him." The lashes of Delaney's closed eyes glistened with unshed tears. "He was a good friend."

Claire's anger turned to regret. Alan had parts of his life he never shared with her because he didn't feel he could. Friends he never spoke of—friends like Ben Delaney. And enemies she didn't know about until it was too late.

One of which was in a room on the floor above. The woman who killed two people and tried to kill a third. The woman who shot her friend could have killed her and her baby. And the woman who orchestrated the murder of her brother.

"I need to use the restroom." Claire walked out of the room as fast as she dared without alerting Jeannie and causing her to question what she was really about to do.

Rage propelled her onto the elevator, where she pushed the button for the third floor. She would find Willa Thoms. All her anxiety over shooting the woman had been replaced by a desire to avenge her brother.

The elevator inched upward from the second to the third floor, giving her plenty of time to rethink her decision. When the doors opened, she took a tentative step out into the hallway. No one was in sight. Any hesitancy she had vanished, and she began her search.

Her phone vibrated in her pocket. Rafe. She pressed the red End button. "Sorry," she said under her breath. A pang of unease hit her. If he knew what she planned to do, he'd stop her. But it wasn't his brother who was murdered.

As she rounded the corner, she stopped and ducked back out of sight. A man in uniform sat outside a doorway halfway down the hall, and this time, she couldn't bluff her way inside. She'd need to use finesse—or deceit. The sign on the door across from her caught her eye. She turned the knob and slipped inside.

A quick search of the shelves yielded a cap Claire used to cover her wavy hair. She buttoned a long blue coat over her clothes and pushed the cleaning cart through the door. When she reached Willa's hospital room, she bent over a mop and headed for the door.

"Let me get that." The guard popped out of his chair and yanked it open. "What happened to the usual lady?"

"Sick," Claire mumbled her answer, head down. Once inside, she waited for the door to close before breathing a sigh of relief. The figure in the bed lay still in the subdued light. Machines with scrolling lines of peaks and valleys softly whirred on either side of the bed.

"If you're here to take more blood, there's none left." The woman's whisper sent a chill through Claire.

"At least you're alive." Claire stepped close to the bed and spit her words out like arrows. "That's more than I can say for my brother, Alan."

"You must be the sister. Too bad I missed."

"Too bad I didn't shoot you through your black heart."

"You here to finish the job?"

Was she? A pillow over her face? An air bubble injected into her IV? Or her hands around the woman's neck, cutting off her air until she ... Claire's stomach lurched, and she bit back a scream of rage.

Claire wished the woman was dead with every atom of her being, but she wouldn't—she couldn't kill her. She snatched the mop from where she'd leaned it against the wall and turned to leave. As she reached the door, she heard Willa speak once more.

"You're just like your brother. Both of you are too soft to finish the job."

Claire dropped the mop and growled deep in her throat. She swung around and covered the distance to the bed in three strides. Willa's eyes gleamed with evil triumph from the pillow.

"Go ahead. Do it." Her raspy whisper snaked around Claire and hissed in her ear.

"Don't. She's not worth losing your soul over." Rafe's words wrapped around her like an invisible shield.

Claire had been focused on the monster in the bed and hadn't heard him enter the room.

Willa gnashed her teeth, her face distorted with hate.

She shrank back from the bed in horror. Rafe pulled her into his arms. "Come on. Let's get out of here." He guided her out the door.

"You'll regret it." Willa spewed hateful curses after them. "You'll see."

"Don't listen to her." Rafe put his mouth close to Claire's ear. "She's going to prison for a very long time."

But something in Claire's spirit told her Willa would never be looking at the world from behind bars.

45

Claire had her hands on Willa's throat when Rafe walked in. Would she have gone through with it? He'd never know, but it was clear that Willa had goaded her into it. For whatever reason, Willa tried to bring Claire down to her level—to make her a killer too. Thank God she hadn't succeeded.

He steered Claire past the officer and down the hall to an empty room. "I understand your anger." He offered her a chair and pulled another over to face her. "I've been there."

She raised her pale face to his. "I don't want to feel like this."

What could he say to wipe away the self-recrimination swimming in her eyes? "All I know is it takes time and prayer." He ignored the dull ache of desire to hold and comfort her. "And the support of your friends."

"But you, Madison and Nate, and Jeannie are the ones who've been there for me. You're my best friends, but soon I'll have to leave. How will I make it without you guys?"

The pain in her voice knifed through Rafe's heart. He couldn't let that happen. "Not if we got married." The words came out soft and slow. His insides churned, and he couldn't look at her. At least she didn't get up and run out of the room. That was a plus.

He'd just about summoned the courage to look her in the eye when she scooted forward and lifted his face to hers.

"I need to be sure about this." She searched his eyes. "Are you asking me to marry you?"

Wasn't that what he'd said? "Yes. I thought—"

She placed a finger over his lips. "Do you love me?"

He pulled her into an embrace, and his lips seized hers with all the love he held for her. Her strong arms pulled him tighter, and she released a little sigh of contentment.

When they finally came up for air, he caressed her cheek with his thumb. "You are the only woman I have ever loved. Marry me."

"Yes, boss." She grinned at him.

"Boss? I can see you and I need to talk before you walk down the aisle." Jeannie stood in the doorway. "Now, do you think you two could give me a moment of your time?"

Rafe glared at Jeannie, but when Claire giggled, he couldn't keep a straight face, and soon, all of them were laughing so hard they were in tears. It was the release they needed.

Wiping her face, Jeannie shook her head. "I'm not sure what I said that was so funny, but okay. Back to business. I understand you two were the last ones to see Willa Thoms alive."

Rafe and Claire stared at her.

"Willa is dead?" The hairs on Claire's arms stood on end.

"She died of what appears to be a heart attack about fifteen minutes ago. The officer outside her room told me about the cleaning lady that went into Thom's room and left in tears with Rafe." Jeannie eyed the disguise Claire still wore.

Claire pulled the paper cap from her head, freeing her auburn waves. "I had to see her—to speak to her. She killed my brother."

"I came looking for Claire." Rafe placed an arm around his recent fiancé. "When we left, Willa was alive and mean as a snake."

"What did she say before Rafe got there?"

Rafe glanced at Claire. Would she tell Jeannie everything?

"I went there full of rage. But when I saw her in the bed, I realized all I wanted was for her to admit she'd arranged to have Alan killed."

"Did she?"

"Yes." Claire ran a hand over her brow.

"Anything about her husband or Irving or Delaney?"

"I didn't mention them. I'm sorry."

Jeannie studied Claire for a moment. "Did you kill Willa Thoms?"

"No." Claire's eyes grew bright with tears. "But I thought about it."

"Okay." Jeannie slapped her notepad shut. "That's enough. Let's get out of here."

"It's been a long day." Rafe ran a hand through his hair without thinking. He winced as his finger caught on the bandage covering his wound. "I'll take you home." He reached for Claire.

"I want to see if Madison is back in her room." She started for the door.

The sting of shame caught him unaware. How could he forget about Madison? He led the way to the elevator.

As they approached the door, he slowed.

"What's wrong?" Claire asked.

"I need a minute." He rubbed his forehead between his eyes.

"I understand. It's tough to see someone you love in pain."

"What if she's lost the baby?" He wasn't sure he could hold it together if that had happened.

"Then she'll need you more than ever. Remember what you said to me? It takes time and prayer and the support of your friends."

He drew her into his arms. She was the missing piece in his life, and he thanked God for bringing her back to him. He kissed her hair.

"Are you two ever coming inside?" Nate smiled at them. "We

recognized your voices and kept waiting for you." He motioned them through the door.

Madison lay snug and secure in the bed, her golden-brown hair fanned out on her pillow and her amber eyes clear and bright. "What were you two talking about out there? Fill me in on the latest."

"Before we do that, how are you?" Claire pulled a chair close to the bed.

"I'm good, and most important, baby Zuberi is too." She patted her stomach. "I'm relegated to bed rest for a couple of days, but that's just a precaution."

Rafe's jaw relaxed. "Here or home?"

"I'll be here tomorrow and hopefully go home the next day."

"Sounds like a plan." Rafe looked at Nate.

The man's thick brown hair was more mussed than usual, and a dark shadow of a beard covered his jaw, but the corners of his mouth were turned up in a smile, and his eyes were filled with joy.

Rafe yawned.

"You two need to get home and rest." Nate stood. "We can talk more tomorrow."

"By the time we get home, it'll almost be tomorrow." Rafe pushed himself to his feet.

"Later then, old man. I'll be sure not to call you too early." Nate uttered a low chuckle. He picked up his phone and looked at the screen. The joy in his eyes faded. "Begay overpowered his guards. He's loose in the hospital."

46

"Jeannie took my gun." Rafe stiffened. "You have one I can use?"

"I'll get you one." Nate checked his own weapon. "Claire, you stay here with Rafe and Madison."

"No." Rafe put a hand on Nate's chest. "I'll go. You stay. You have more to lose." He cut his eyes to Claire. Would she understand? "Give me a gun."

"I can't let you do this."

"I'm going, gun or no gun." Rafe marched toward the door.

"Wait." Nate caught up to him. He opened it and checked the hall. An officer stood near the nurse's station. "Come here." He motioned to the man. "Do you have a second weapon on you?"

The officer blushed. "Sir, I ..."

"You're not in trouble, but I need it." Nate waggled his fingers.

The officer pulled up his pant leg and withdrew a small pistol. He handed it to Nate.

Nate checked the gun. "Any more ammo?"

He dropped seven bullets into Nate's hand.

"You know Eugene Begay is loose in the hospital."

"Yes, sir."

"I'll be in my wife's hospital room with another friend. I'm armed, so don't barge in." Nate placed a hand on his shoulder. "I want you to keep guard out here."

"Yes, sir." The officer straightened. "I won't let him past me."

Rafe looked at the young man and prayed he wouldn't get hurt.

Nate patted the officer's shoulder and returned to Madison's room. Rafe followed.

"Here." Nate handed him the gun and the extra bullets. "You have my permission to use deadly force if necessary."

Rafe stuffed the small gun in his waistband and the ammo in his pocket. He checked his phone battery. Low, but it would have to do. "Let me know if you get any intel on his whereabouts."

Nate nodded.

"If you die, I'll never forgive you." Claire grabbed him by the front of his shirt.

"Is that code for I love you?"

"Yes." She kissed him hard on the lips and let him go.

Rafe slipped out the door into the hall. "It's me, officer. Don't shoot."

"Yes, sir."

He'd take the stairs. But should he go up or down? In the stairwell, Rafe stood still and let his pulse slow until he could hear past the blood rushing in his ears. Was that a footstep? Was the big man light on his feet? Or was it a police officer?

Getting shot by Begay wasn't his only worry. He could get shot by a friendly—another good guy in search of the big man too. Hopefully, Nate called whoever was in charge and let them know he was out here. But when adrenaline ran high, mistakes got made.

Another footstep. Followed by a muttered curse. Rafe took out his phone and texted Nate. He made sure his phone was on vibrate. The last thing he needed was the James Bond theme echoing in the stairwell. The footsteps seemed to come from above his head. He moved to the staircase and put his foot on the bottom step. The industrial staircase was built with open spaces between the risers.

As he climbed the stairs, Rafe peered up between the steps for a glimpse of a pant leg or shoe. He reached the first landing and crouched. If Begay was inside the stairwell on the third floor, Rafe should see him when he peeked above the railing.

He prepared himself for quick action and raised his head, leveling his gun at the space above him. No Begay. Rafe ducked back down. Could he have been wrong? Could the footsteps have been below him?

A movement to his right caught his eye, and he realized his mistake. The stairs continued up another level. A shot rang out. Searing pain pulsed through his right arm, and he tumbled down three steps before catching the railing with his left hand.

His gun lay on the landing above him. He needed to get to it right away if he had any hope of surviving. He gritted his teeth against the pain and crawled back to the landing. "One, two, three," he whispered before lunging for the gun and rolling across the landing until he was directly under Begay. The pain from that maneuver left him lightheaded.

Shots pinged off metal as Begay attempted to finish what he'd started. Rafe raised his left hand and aimed, forcing his eyes to focus. His shot missed. The big man bounded down the stairs and jumped onto the landing in front of Rafe.

"Your police buddy isn't here to save you this time." Begay raised his gun. Pointed at Rafe. And pulled the trigger. The hammer clicked on an empty chamber. With a roar, he ran at Rafe.

Rafe fired his gun. The big man stumbled backward. When he hit the railing, the momentum of his bulk carried him over, and he fell three stories to the concrete below.

Lances of stabbing pain ran up Rafe's arm from his elbow to

his shoulder. He tried to sit up but collapsed, panting, on the floor.

The stairwell filled with noise. Doors opened on all levels, and men poured in. Their shouts echoed throughout the concrete and metal shaft.

"Quiet." Jeannie's commanding voice rose above the din. "Rafe, where are you?"

He pulled in a big breath and tried to speak. Nothing came out. He shifted position, drew in a breath, and yelled. "Here." Exhausted, he closed his eyes and prayed.

"I think I heard him." Jeannie climbed the steps two at a time. "Get a doc."

47

Claire stretched and caught herself before falling off the sofa. Where was she? She shifted her gaze around the room until it landed on the hospital bed. Rafe's profile brought everything rushing back along with all the initial anxiety. She swallowed the stomach acid that threatened to rise in her throat and sat up. Looking at Rafe once more, she uttered a short prayer of thanks.

Tears pricked her eyes. Rafe was her protector, her strong man. He wasn't supposed to be lying in a hospital bed with tubes in his arm and his nose. The scene brought back memories of her brother, David.

She drew in a deep breath. But Rafe wasn't dying. He was wounded, and he would mend. She only had to be strong for him for a little while. Then life would be back the way it should be.

The door opened. "You have some visitors, Mr. O'Connell." The nurse swept into the room and checked the monitors. "How do you feel?"

A flicker of a smile appeared on Rafe's face. "Great." He tugged his left arm out from under the covers. "Claire?"

"I'm here." She jumped up and took his hand. The strength of his grip brought a sigh of thanksgiving to her lips.

His smile widened.

"So, Rafe." Jeannie's unmistakable voice preceded her into the room. "You just couldn't stand that Madison was getting all the attention, could you?"

His smile turned into a grin.

"Give the man a break." Nate entered next—pushing a wheelchair.

"Madison." Claire dropped Rafe's hand and rushed to her friend. "What are you doing out of bed?"

Nate rolled her over to where Claire had been standing.

"The doctor said I could come for a visit as long as I didn't make it too long." She touched Rafe's hand. "I hear I almost lost you, bro. Again. You've got to stop doing this to me."

"I'll try." The breathing tube from the operation on his elbow had left his voice warped and rusty.

"We came to give you the latest news." Nate motioned for Claire to take a seat. "We'll do the talking, so you don't have to. Jeannie, why don't you start?"

"Okay." She pulled her notepad from her purse. "First, Eugene Begay lived long enough after his fall to confess to killing Alan Green. Second, Bulldog—Randy—opened the rest of the files on the flash drive and found all the evidence we need to wrap up the prostitution ring."

"What about Henry Young, the boss?" Claire asked. "And the Folly brothers?"

"Kent and Lenard Folly have been charged with attempted kidnapping and attempted theft." Nate pulled a chair between Madison and Claire. "They've agreed to testify against Henry Young for kidnapping charges and the theft, but they have no first-hand knowledge of him trying to kill Ben Delaney."

"Wasn't he wearing the same shoes as Kent?" Frustration simmered inside Claire.

"Too circumstantial." Nate shook his head. "But we'll keep interviewing Young. He'll cave eventually."

"Was he working for Begay?"

"We think so."

"And Begay was working for Allie, a.k.a. Willa Thoms."

"Apparently."

"I still don't understand what started it all." Claire's irritation level continued to climb.

"I think I do," Madison spoke for the first time. "I believe that when Mathis Thoms found out about her continued involvement with the prostitution ring, he gave her an ultimatum. Either stop, or he'd blow the whistle."

"Maybe she promised to stop to shut him up." Jeannie perched on the end of Rafe's bed. "But when Tommy or Mathis or whoever he was figured out the truth, he told Ben Delaney who told Alan."

"Yes." Nate picked up the thread. "She needed to get away, but her money was tied up in the offshore account that Begay had access to. If she wanted to reinvent herself for good, the first thing she had to do was to get rid of everyone who knew anything about her true identity. Starting with her husband."

"Then Alan and the others." Claire leaned forward. "But where does Begay come in?"

"That's easy. She intended to use him to do her dirty work and get to the money. He hired Henry Young, who brought in the Folly brothers. When she didn't need him any longer ..." Jeannie pulled her hand across her throat. "Off with his head."

"He was, as they say, a dead man walking." Madison sighed. "So many deaths and attempted murders." She placed a hand on her abdomen.

"I think it's back to bed for you, darlin'." Nate rose and took hold of the wheelchair handles. "We'll see you tomorrow, Rafe."

"I'll come visit you." He forced the words out and coughed.

"Uh-huh." Madison gave him a sideways look. "For once, do as you're told."

"I'll make sure he does." Claire gave him a stern look.

Rafe rolled his eyes.

"Sorry, man, can't help you." Nate gave him a half-cocked smile. "It's two against one."

"Let me get the door." Jeannie hurried over. "I'll be right back."

Claire took Rafe's hand again. He turned his face to hers with his chiseled jaw and eyes the color of a blue flame—the hottest burning flame there is. For the first time, she noticed flecks of gold amidst the blue. Like rays of sunlight shining from deep inside. "You have the most beautiful eyes."

"You." He raised his hand, still entwined with hers, and pointed to her.

Claire stared at their hands, and she knew deep in her being what she wanted more than anything. "Let's get married."

Rafe furrowed his brow at her and shook their hands.

"I know we're engaged, but I'm talking about right now. Here. They have pastors at hospitals, don't they?" Claire picked up Rafe's call button. "What do you say? We can have a big party for all our friends and family later."

He stared at her for a long moment. Then he nodded.

"What did I miss?" Jeannie barged in and swung her gaze from Rafe to Claire and back.

48

Christmas Day

Claire watched through the back window of the rental as Madison and the twins glided over the ice behind their house. Rafe wrapped his left arm around her from behind.

"I know it's hard for you. Living here. But it's only until we find a place of our own." He kissed her cheek.

"I don't mind." She hugged his arm. "I love being next door to Madison and Nate and the twins, and living on the lake is wonderful. I could stay here." She peered around. "If we change some of the furniture."

"Fair enough." He released her. "Who's going to be at Nate and Madison's today?"

"Zoe and Peter. Your Aunt Sarah and Uncle Ed. Bernadette and Daniel, and Daniel's Aunt Rose. And us. I think that's it. Jeannie is going to Bill's family to celebrate."

"When are we supposed to be there?"

"In two hours."

"Good." He waggled his eyebrows at her.

"I have a green bean casserole to make." She held up a hand.

"Besides, you're in a sling for two more weeks. Remember? Watch a football game, sweetheart."

He eased his arm around her waist again. "Aren't we newlyweds?" He nuzzled her neck.

"Yes." She slipped away from him with her sweetest smile. "But we'll have to postpone our newlywed celebrations until you're fully healed."

Claire grinned inside at the normality of it all. This is what she'd been missing all those years. Someone to love and who loved her back. Friends, a community, roots, and most importantly, hope. She touched the cross necklace Madison had given her as a wedding present.

"Alan," she said under her breath. "I hope you can see all the good that came from what you did." She placed her fingertips on his photo. "In the process, you lost your life. But it wasn't in vain. I love you, and I'm proud of you. Goodbye, bro."

ACKNOWLEDGMENTS

I always find it a bit overwhelming when I think about who I want to thank for helping me put together a book. How can I adequately express my gratitude and humility?

First, there are my readers—those of you who support my work and ask for the next book. You have no idea how much that means to an author like me. Thank you.

A big thanks to CW3 Larry Myers, US Army (Ret.), who once again shared his 30+ years of experience in criminal investigation in the Army CID, Tennessee Bureau of Investigation, and Criminal Investigation for the Department of Justice to help me with police procedure. I am proud to call him and his wonderful wife, Nancy, friends.

Let me say here that I take full responsibility for any problems you may have with the actions of my characters or mistakes you find in the book. Imagination is a wonderful thing. But it can get you into trouble.

My Word Weaver posse—Bonnie Sue Beardsley, Starr Ayers, Denise Holmberg, Linda Dindzans, Caroline Powers, and Charlsie Estess—keeps me on track. Their support and encouragement keep me striving to be a better writer and a better person.

Many thanks to DiAnn Mills, my friend and mentor, who is always there when I need her.

And Patricia Bradley, my friend and encourager.

Along with all the wonderful people I've already mentioned, I have found a second family in Scrivenings Press with Linda

Fulkerson and all the amazing authors there. She has not only created an excellent publishing house but a family of Christian authors full of support and love, who lift up each other.

Above all else, I thank God, who determines our steps and brings us together. And especially for the gift of my husband, Les, the love of my life, my biggest fan and supporter.

ABOUT DEBORAH SPRINKLE

Deborah Sprinkle could start her bio with, "When she's not hiking or white water rafting, Deborah is writing ..." but it wouldn't be true. She used to do those things, but that was a long time ago. And somehow, "When she's not napping" doesn't have the same ring. Deborah *can* tell you she's a retired research chemist and chemistry teacher turned award-winning author with seven books to her name and more coming. All romantic suspense and mysteries. She's also a wife, mom, and grandmother and lives in Memphis with her wonderful husband of 50+ years.

MORE FROM THE TROUBLE IN PLEASANT VALLEY SERIES

Deadly Guardian

Trouble in Pleasant Valley—*Book One*

Madison Long, a high school chemistry teacher, looks forward to a relaxing summer break. Instead, she suffers through a nightmare of threats, terror, and death. When she finds a man murdered she once dated, Detective Nate Zuberi is assigned to the case, and in the midst of chaos, attraction blossoms into love.

Together, she and Nate search for her deadly guardian before he decides the only way to truly save her from what he considers a hurtful relationship is to kill her—and her policeman boyfriend as well.

Get your copy here:

https://scrivenings.link/deadlyguardian

Death of an Imposter

Trouble in Pleasant Valley—*Book Two*

Her first week on the job and rookie detective Bernadette Santos has been given the murder of a prominent citizen to solve. But when her victim turns out to be an imposter, her straight forward case takes a nasty turn. One that involves the attractive Dr. Daniel O'Leary, a visitor to Pleasant Valley and a man harboring secrets.

When Dr. O'Leary becomes a target of violence himself, Detective Santos has two mysteries to unravel. Are they related? And how far can she trust the good doctor? Her heart tugs her one way while her mind pulls her another. She must discover the solutions before it's too late!

Get your copy here:

https://scrivenings.link/deathofanimposter

Silence Can Be Deadly

Trouble in Pleasant Valley—*Book Three*

Forced from the career he loved and into driving a taxi, Peter Grace had grown accustomed to his simple life. Until one night when a suspicious fare and a traffic jam blew it all apart, and he was on the run again. Only this time it wasn't a matter of changing occupations but of life and death.

He needed help and he knew where to find it. His old friend Rafe in Pleasant Valley. What he didn't count on was finding not only the help he needed but a community of new friends and the love of his life. Zoe Poole.

The story of Captain Nate Zuberi and his wife Madison continues as they, too, risk their lives to help Peter. Along with Peter, Rafe, and Zoe, they strive to catch an assassin.

But can the group of friends find the killer before anyone else gets hurt?

Get your copy here:

https://scrivenings.link/silencecanbedeadly

MAC & SAM MYSTERIES

The Case of the Innocent Husband

A Mac & Sam Mystery—Book One

Private Investigator Mackenzie Love needs to do one thing. Find out who shot Eleanor Davis. Or she'll have to leave town.

When Eleanor Davis is found shot in her garage, the only suspect, her estranged husband, is found not guilty in a court of law. However, most of the good citizens of Washington, Missouri, remain unconvinced. It doesn't matter that twelve men and women of the jury found him not guilty. What do they know?

And since Private Investigator Mackenzie Love accepted the job for the defense and helped acquit Connor Davis, her friends and neighbors have placed her squarely in the enemy camp. Therefore, her overwhelming goal becomes to find out who killed Eleanor Davis.

Or leave the town she grew up in.

As the investigation progresses, the threats escalate. Someone wants to stop Mackenzie and her partner, Samantha Majors, and is willing to do whatever it takes—including murder.

Can Mac and Sam find the killer before they each end up on the wrong side of a bullet?

Get your copy here:

https://scrivenings.link/innocenthusband

The Case of Mistaken Identity

A Mac & Sam Mystery—Book Two

Private Investigator Mackenzie Love manages to get into trouble on a simple shopping trip where she finds herself at the business end of a gun. It's clear her attacker mistakes her for someone else, but who? And why is her look-alike in so much trouble?

Mac enlists the help of her partners, Samantha Majors and Miss P, and Detective Jake Sanders to find her doppelgänger and solve the case of mistaken identity.

In the meantime, Mr. Fischer of Fischer Industries comes to the private detectives for help with a problem of his own. As Mac and Sam work on his case, they begin to wonder if the two cases are related.

Can Mac and Sam unravel the clues and get justice for both Mac's look-alike and Mr. Fischer?

Get your copy here:

https://scrivenings.link/mistakenidentity

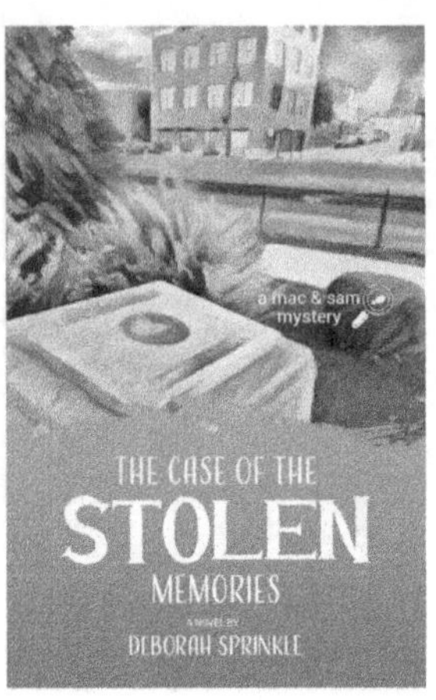

The Case of the Stolen Memories

A Mac & Sam Mystery—Book Three

It's the beginning of a new year and Private Investigator Mackenzie Love resolves to get in better shape. But after only one week of walking before work, she interrupts a burglary in progress and ends up in the middle of a murder case.

Detective Jake Sanders, the man Mac's dating, is assigned to the murder, and Mac, along with her partners Samantha Majors and Ms. Prudence Freebody, are hired to find the memorabilia stolen from the time capsule in Rennick Park. The two cases intertwine, and Mac finds herself once more on the wrong end of a gun!

Can Mac and Jake find the killer and the stolen property before the killer finds them?

Get your copy here:

https://scrivenings.link/stolenmemories

Sharktooth Island

A collection of Romantic Suspense novellas

A fabled island that no one dares to tame.

This collection contains four novellas:

Book 1 - Out of the Storm (*1830*) by Susan Page Davis

Laura Bryant sails with her father and his three-man crew on his small coastal trading schooner. After a short stay in Jamaica, where she meets Alex Dryden, an officer on another ship, the Bryants set out for their home in New England.

In a storm, they are blown off course east of Savannah, Georgia, to a foreboding island. Captain Bryant tells his daughter he's heard tales of that isle. It's impossible to land on, though it looks green and inviting from a distance. It has no harbor but is surrounded by dangerous rocks and cliffs.

Pirates outrun the storm and decide to bury a cache of treasure on this island and return for it later. On board is Alex, whom the cutthroats captured in Jamaica and forced to work for them. Alex risks his own life to escape the pirates and tries to help Laura and Captain Bryant outwit them. Beneath the deadly struggle, romance blossoms for Laura.

Book 2 - *A Passage of Chance* (1893) by Linda Fulkerson

Orphaned at a young age, Melody Lampert longs to escape the loveless home of the grandmother who begrudgingly raised her. Stripped of her inheritance due to her grandmother's resentments, Melody discovers her name remains on the deed of one property—an obscure island off the Georgia coast that she shares with her cousin. But when he learns the island may contain a hidden pirate treasure, he's determined to cheat her out of her share.

Ship's mechanic Padric Murphy made a vow to his dying father—break the curse that has plagued their family for generations. To do so, he must return what was taken from Sharktooth Island decades earlier—a pair of rare gold pieces. His opportunity to right the wrong arrives when his new employer sets sail to explore the island.

After a series of unexplainable mishaps occur, endangering Padric and his boss's beautiful cousin Melody, he fears his chance of breaking the curse may be ruined. But is the island's greed thwarting his plans? Or the greed of someone else?

Book 3 - *Island Mayhem* (1937) by Elena Hill

Louise Krause stopped piloting to pursue nursing, but when money got too tight she was forced to give up her dreams and start ferrying around a playboy who managed to excel during the Great Depression. When a routine aerial tour turns south, Louise is unable to save the plane.

After crash landing, the cocky pilot is stranded. She longs to escape the uninhabited island, but her makeshift raft sinks, and she and her companions are in even worse trouble. Can Louise learn to trust the others in order to survive, or will the island's curse and potential sabotage lead to her demise?

Book 4 - *After the Storm* (*present day*) by Deborah Sprinkle

Mercedes Baxter inherited two passions from her father—a love for Sharktooth Island, a spit of land in the middle of the ocean left to her in his will, and a dedication to the study of the flora and fauna on and around its rocky landscape.

For the last five years, since graduating from college, Mercy led a peaceful, simple life on the island with only her cat, Hawkeye, for company. Through grant money she obtained from a conservancy in Savannah, she could live on her island while studying and writing about the plants and animals there. Life was perfect.

But when a hurricane hits the island, Mercy's life changes for good. Her high school sweetheart, Liam Stewart, shows up to help her with repairs, and ignites the flame that has never quite died away. And if that's not enough, while assessing the damage to the island, they make a discovery that puts both their lives in danger.

Stay up-to-date on your favorite books and authors with our free e-newsletters.

ScriveningsPress.com